THE STORE

Also by James Patterson

JAMES PATTERSON
& RICHARD DiLALLO
THE STORE

CENTURY

1 3 5 7 9 10 8 6 4 2

Century
20 Vauxhall Bridge Road
London SW1V 2SA

Century is part of the Penguin Random House group of companies
whose addresses can be found at global.penguinrandomhouse.com.

Penguin
Random House
UK

First published by Century in 2017

www.penguin.co.uk

A CIP catalogue record for this book is available from the British Library.

ISBN 9781780895338
ISBN 9781780895345 (export edition)

Printed and bound by in Great Britain by Clays Ltd, St Ives Plc

Penguin Random House is committed to a sustainable future
for our business, our readers and our planet. This book is made
from Forest Stewardship Council® certified paper.

MIX
Paper from
responsible sources
FSC
www.fsc.org   FSC® C018179

For my sister Maryellen—who's always had my back since the 1950s. Love you.

THE STORE

THE STORE

PROLOGUE

ONE

I CAN'T stop running. Not now. Not ever.

I think the police are following me. Unless they're not.

That's the crazy part. I'm just not sure.

Maybe somebody recognized me...

My picture's been all over. I bet someone called the NYPD and said, "There's a crazy guy, about forty-five years old, stumbling around SoHo. On Prince Street. Wild-man eyes. You'd better get him before he hurts himself."

They always say that—"before he hurts himself." Like they care.

That crazy guy is me. And if *I* had seen me, I would have called the cops, too. My dirty-blond hair really *is* dirty and sweaty from running. The rest of me? I feel like hell and look worse. Torn jeans (not hip, just torn), dirty army-green T-shirt, dirty classic red-and-white Nikes. "Dirty" is the theme. But it doesn't really matter.

All that matters right now is the box I'm carrying. A cardboard box, held together with pieces of string. What's in it? A four-hundred-and-ten-page manuscript.

I keep running. I look around. So this is what SoHo's become...neat and clean and very rich. Give the people what they want. And what they want is SoHo as a tourist attraction—high-tech gyms and upscale restaurants. Not much else. The cool "buy-in-bulk" underwear shops and electronics stores selling 1950s lighting fixtures have all disappeared. Today you can buy a five-hundred-dollar dinner of porcini mushroom foam with frozen nettle crème brûlée, but you can't buy a pair of Jockey shorts or a Phillips-head screwdriver or a quart of skim milk.

I stop for a moment in front of a restaurant—the sign says PORC ET FLAGEOLETS. The translation is high school easy—"pork and beans." Adorable. Just then I hear a woman's voice behind me.

"That's gotta be him. That's the guy. Jacob Brandeis."

I turn around. The woman is "old" SoHo—black tights, tattoos, Native American silver jewelry. Eighty years old at least. Her tats have wrinkles. She must have lived in SoHo since the Dutch settled New York.

"I'm going to call the police," she says. She's not afraid of me.

Her equally hip but much younger male friend says, "Let's not. Who the hell wants to get involved?"

They deliberately cross the street, and I hear the woman speak. "I have to say: he is really handsome."

That comment doesn't surprise me. Women like me a lot. Okay, that's obnoxious and arrogant, but it's true. The old gal should have seen me a few years ago. I had long dirty-blond hair, and, as a girl in college once told me, I was a "hunky nerd." I was. Until all this shit happened to me and wore me out and brought me down and . . .

The old lady and younger man are now across the street. I shout to them.

"You don't have to call the cops, lady. I'm sure they know I'm here."

As if to prove this fact to myself, I look up and see a camera-packed drone hovering above me, recording my every step. How could I have forgotten? Drones zoom through the sky—in pairs, in groups, alone. Tiny cameras dot the corners of every building. In this New York, a person is never really alone.

I stumble along for another block, then I stop at a classic SoHo cast-iron building. It's home to Writers Place, the last major publisher left in New York. Hell, it's the last major publisher in all of America.

I clutch the box that holds the manuscript. Dirt streaks my face. My back and armpits are soaked. You know you smell like hell when you can smell your own sweat.

I'm about to push my way through the revolving door when I pause.

I feel like I could cry, but instead I extend the middle finger of my right hand and flip it at the drone.

TWO

ANNE GUTMAN, editor in chief and publisher of Writers Place, greets me with her usual warmth.

"You look like shit," she says.

"Thank you," I say. "Now let's get the hell out of your office and go someplace where we can't be watched."

"Where'd you have in mind, Jacob? Jupiter or Mars?"

"Christ. I can't stand it," I say. "They watch me 24-7."

She nods, but I'm not sure she agrees with me. I'm not even sure she cares. I lean forward and hand her the box.

"What's this?" she says. "A gift?"

"It's the manuscript! It's *Twenty-Twenty*!" I yell. Why am I yelling?

Anne tosses her head back and laughs.

"I can't remember the last time I received a hard-copy manuscript," she says.

Then I look at her intently. I lower my voice.

"Look, Anne. This book is incredible. This is corporate reporting like it's never been written before."

"You know my concern, Jacob," she says.

"Yeah. I know. You don't think the Store is worth writing about; you don't truly think it's morally bankrupt."

"That's not it. I think it may very well be morally bankrupt, but I can make a list of forty companies that are just as bad. I don't think the Store is *inherently* evil. It's a creative monopoly."

"Read my book. Read *Twenty-Twenty*. Then decide."

"I will."

"Tonight?" I ask.

"Yes. Tonight. Immediately."

"Immediately? Wow. That's fast."

Anne smiles at my minuscule joke. I try to remain calm. I'm sure if she reads the book she's going to be blown away. Then again, maybe she won't be. Maybe she'll toss it after a few chapters. What do I know? After all, I've been wrong about this sort of thing before.

Suddenly there's noise. A scuffling of feet. Indistinguishable but loud. It comes from outside Anne's office. Then a very quick knock on the door. Before Anne can say anything, her assistant opens the door and speaks.

"Ms. Gutman, there are three policemen and two NYPD detectives out here with me."

"What do they want?" Anne asks.

"They're here to arrest Mr. Brandeis."

Anne and I look at each other as her assistant closes the door. I'm about to fall apart. As always, she's in take-charge mode.

"You go out through the conference room. Then take the back stairs down and outside. Find a place to stay."

Anne hands me some money from the top drawer of her desk. I turn toward the conference room.

"I'll handle the cops," Anne says.

"Read the book, okay?" I say.

"Damn it, Jacob. Of course I'll read the book."

She walks out her office door. I also start walking. The last thing I hear her say is: "Good afternoon, officers. How can I help you?"

EIGHT MONTHS EARLIER

CHAPTER 1

MY WIFE, Megan, wrote an e-vite to our dinner party that was like Megan herself: funny, sharp, and a touch mysterious:

MEGAN AND JACOB BRANDEIS

INVITE YOU TO OUR

"LAST GASP IN MANHATTAN" PARTY

TUESDAY EVENING, AUGUST 30

8:00 P.M.

322 PEARL STREET

We had invited our eight best friends to have dinner with us in the big goofy-looking loft space that we had carved out of half a floor in an art deco building. If you're thinking when you hear the word *loft* that the space was glamorous, high-tech, and modern, you're thinking wrong. Our very long, very narrow apartment was in what had once been an old insurance company building. After that, it was vacant for five years. Then it was home to a bunch of squatters. Then it was bought by a bunch of would-be writers and artists. Each apartment had a *tiny* view of the East River and a *fabulous* view of the garbage barges docked at the South Street Seaport. We could afford the apartment only because the area at the time (then the Financial District, now very chicly called FiDi) was a no-man's-land. The nearest grocery store was two miles away in Greenwich Village. We could also afford it because we were making *fairly* decent money writing everything from ad copy to catalog copy to an occasional piece for *New York* magazine and the *New York Observer*. Like everyone else in Manhattan who hadn't founded a tech company or managed a hedge fund, we made do. What's even better is that our kids seemed to have no problem making do.

Lindsay was sixteen and attended Spence. When I was a kid at George Washington High, Spence was debutante-snooty. Only a touch of that culture remained, and those types didn't seem to interest Lindsay. In fact, most of her friends seemed to be the Latinos and African American scholarship kids, with a UN ambassador's daughter or Middle Eastern princess thrown in for diversity.

Alex, Lindsay's thirteen-year-old brother, attended a Reform-Jewish prep school, Rodeph Sholom, on the Upper West Side. He pretty much liked his school and liked his friends and didn't hate the subway ride up to the place. We had sent him there because both Megan and I were thoroughly unreligious—she a lapsed Catholic, I a Jew in terms of culture only. But by the end of his first month at the school, Alex had become almost frighteningly interested in Judaism. He studied as much Torah as he did computer science. He studied Chinese, but he also took Hebrew. And of course he made me feel embarrassed that my knowledge of Judaism revolved around three things: (1) food (matzo balls should be hard), (2) superstitions that no other Jewish family had ever heard of ("Touch a coat button if you see a nun"), and (3) the words *be careful,* which we say to anyone leaving our apartment—a plumber, a great-aunt, a Jehovah's Witness.

Alex and Lindsay fought constantly with each other, and when they weren't fighting they were laughing with each other. Plus they read books—real books with real paper pages that you have to use your fingers to turn. These kids were smart, sarcastic, and usually nice. Megan and I really got a kick out of them. I don't want to speculate how much they reciprocated the adoration.

The evening of the party found Megan and me very nervous. But we had our reasons. I poured Megan her third white wine (an unusually enormous amount for her), and Lindsay and Alex put the final touches on the dinner—Lindsay glazed the poached salmon while Alex scattered the watercress over the fish. "I'm doing watercress. Dill is a catering cliché." Great chefs talk tough.

"Live and learn," I said.

Megan took a sip of her wine and spoke. "Maybe we should have entitled this evening the 'Last Dinosaurs in Manhattan' party."

I laughed and said, "Maybe," but I knew what she meant. All eight guests were people whose jobs were simply not very important anymore. In a piece I had written the previous month for Salon.com, I had referred to this category of worker as "leftover people in our new high-tech world."

Yes, the friends who'd be eating our salmon that evening were folks waiting to be—as the British would say—"made redundant." I had been thinking of that scene in the movie *The Tall Guy* in which the boss turns to his assistant, played by Jeff Goldblum, and says, "You're fired. F-U-C-K-E-D. Fired!" If I sound heartless, I don't mean to be. It was a fact of life, and it was happening all over the country.

The night was a kind of debutante party for those "coming out" of the workforce.

Sandi Feinblum, the assistant style editor at the *New York Times*, was taking a buyout. She had been assigned to the "traditional" hard-copy newspaper. But the only people who still preferred the printed *Times* were slowly but surely showing up on the obituaries page.

Wendy Witten and Chuck McKirdy were editors of a wine magazine and a golf magazine respectively; neither publication had transitioned successfully from a news-stand presence to an Internet presence.

We had also invited an executive from Sotheby's auction house and his very nervous, prescription-druggy wife. He was quickly being strangled into oblivion by websites like eBay and iGavel.

One woman had already gotten the ax. A former travel agent. All the people who once used her services were now making their own hotel reservations and printing their own airline tickets. In essence, she had been replaced by William Shatner.

One guy, Charlie Burke, was in a business that was about to be eaten by Fox. When that meal took place, he would probably be known as the last guy on earth who had ever managed an independent broadcasting company. His syndicated sitcoms would be just another part of neocon broadcasting.

And finally there was Anne Gutman, editor in chief of Writers Place. Anne still managed to make a living editing and occasionally publishing a few nonfiction writers such as Megan and me. But she knew—we all knew—that she was the exception to the electronic rule.

Shit. The unemployment office could have set up an application desk in our dining room. What's more, Megan and I would have been first in line.

CHAPTER 2

YES, WE were in trouble.

From the outside we still looked prosperous—the crazy-looking loft (full of interesting, artsy "found objects"), the two good-looking teenage kids, the August rental on Fire Island.

But the fact was, we were hurting badly.

To our shock, Anne Gutman had turned down the book that Megan and I had been working on for almost two years. Our proposed project was entitled *The Roots of Rap*. It traced the history of rap music from blues through early rock and roll, then doo-wop, and ultimately the past twenty-five years of rap and hip-hop.

"I just don't have the funds anymore," Anne had said. "I had money when you started the project, but I've just been squeezed too hard by the Internet....Then, of course, there's always the Store....I just can't afford to take big risks anymore....I could shove it into self-publish, but the guys in research told me you'd be lucky to sell five hundred copies."

The Store. This online colossus was becoming a huge player in the world of publishing. And in every other part of the consumer world as well.

The Store stocked what people wanted. Then, because it controlled pricing, it pretty much told us what to buy. It's where we all went shopping for our toasters, tractors, Tide, soy sauce, jeans, lightbulbs. If somebody on earth manufactured something, anything, the Store sold it. Potted oak trees, cases of wine, automobiles...all usually at a lower price than the brick-and-mortar source.

The Store's publishing arm was churning out e-books, and every once in a while they'd hit upon something really popular. *Okay*, Megan and I thought...*if you can't beat 'em*...

So as soon as the painful impact of Anne's rejection sank in, we did the only thing left to do. We moved over to the opposition: we flipped open our laptops, quickly pulled up the Store page, then clicked over to "Independent Publishing." We had no other choice. Why the hell not? Megan and I were sure we had a bestselling e-book.

Within less than a *minute* of logging on, I was having my first e-mail conversation with my "contact rep."

At the beginning, our e-mail conversations were all warm hugs and wet kisses. A few rewrites. Our promise to start a Twitter account, a Facebook page, an Instagram profile—the usual social-media journey to the bestseller list. It was going great...only a matter of time until Megan and I would be looking at book-cover concepts.

Then came the not-so-inevitable kick in the balls.

With one tap of the Send button, the Store destroyed

our plan. They suddenly rejected *The Roots of Rap*. No reason was given. Their e-mail sounded like a ransom letter: *Your project is no longer viable. The Store.*

My index finger raced to the Reply tab. *Hey, folks, what gives? All of a sudden? This idea is a winner waiting to happen. This book could really live online. It's about music. You know, music downloads. The YouTube clips. The cross-ref . . .*

Came a one-line response: *We are as sorry about the outcome as you are. The Store.*

It was clear: the Store was finished with us. Or so they thought.

But *we* were not finished with the Store. Not by a long shot.

CHAPTER 3

"NEBRASKA! THAT'S nuts!" Chuck McKirdy shouted. "You two will be moving to freakin' Nebraska?"

Megan stepped in and answered the question with her usual patience.

"That's where the jobs are. So that's where we'll be going," she said softly.

"What's Nebraska's nickname? The Cornhusking State?" Sandi asked.

I corrected her. "The Cornhusker State."

"Go, Cornhuskers!" someone shouted.

The chant was quickly picked up. "Go, Cornhuskers! Go, Cornhuskers!"

"Okay," I said. "The annual asshole convention will now come to order."

Megan smiled, then began a little speech. She said it was hardly a secret in our social group that our most recent nonfiction effort had been rejected "not merely by faithful friends who shall remain nameless"—at this point Anne Gutman jokingly hid her face behind her unfolded napkin—"but also...and you're not going to believe this humiliation...even rejected by the Store.

"So with *The Roots of Rap* totally without a future, and Jacob and I—not to mention our two kids—totally without a future, it looked like we were doomed. But just when things looked darkest, lo and behold, the Store came through for us."

We stopped talking. Just for a moment, but long enough to run the risk of screwing up our story. And it was a story, almost a fairy tale. It was a highly fictionalized account of what had really happened.

At that very moment Megan and I were about to tell a very big lie to our closest friends. And even though we had rehearsed it carefully, my stomach was rolling, my chest was filling with acid, and Megan's hands visibly shook. But the starting pistol had been fired. We had to talk. So Megan took off.

"Well, it's sort of crazy what happened next. We thought it was all finished between us and the Store. And Alex and Lindsay even started joking about being so poor that they'd have to decide which relatives to go live with."

I interrupted. "Nobody wanted to go with Megan's family."

She punched me gently. (We had not rehearsed the ad-libs.)

"Anyway, we got a message from the Store HR people, and they...offered...us...jobs."

"Doing what?" Chuck asked. "Writing ad copy or catalog stuff?"

"Well, that's the sorry part," I said. "They're kinda

crappy jobs. We'll be working in their fulfillment center. You know, filling orders and getting them out to people. But . . ." I paused. I was lost.

Megan was not going to let that sentence hang there in space. "But," Megan said, "because the Store is so big and growing, we'll be eligible for promotions and advancements within three months. Just three months."

"And that's the story," I said, hoping that the strength in my delivery would let me recover and seal the deal with my friends.

Okay, they were surprised. Very surprised. And yes, our friends were still spitting out a few farmer jokes, a few Republican jokes, a few Cornhusker jokes. But as I looked around the room I could tell everyone believed me. Someone mentioned a good-bye party. Someone else mentioned a group bus trip to Nebraska. Yes, it looked like everyone believed us.

Well, almost everyone.

I glanced out the apartment window and saw a drone hovering. It was recording everything going on at our dinner table.

I also noticed that Anne Gutman was looking directly at me. We were good friends, old friends. She had a weak smile on her lips. And I could tell that Anne wasn't buying a single word of our story.

CHAPTER 4

OKAY, WE had told our friends a lie. But it wasn't a total lie. I say that as if a partial lie is somehow more acceptable.

Yes, we were moving to Nebraska. Yes, we were going to work at the Store. But here's what we left out:

The Store had not invited us to work there.

The real truth was that Megan and I had made all this happen. And like a lot of things, it all started with a simple idea.

Here's how the bean stalk grew: after the Store had rejected our manuscript, I was burning with anger and resentment. Sure, they thought they could screw me. Well, here's some news. I was going to show them. If I sound like a crazy person, I think it's because I was.

Megan and I would infiltrate the Store. We'd unearth their secrets and their plans. Then we'd write about it. We'd get even. But first we had to get hired.

Some good news (finally): it turned out that getting hired by the Store was incredibly easy. The Store's business was growing so fast that apparently they accepted almost everyone who clicked on the link that sat at the bottom of every Store Web page: "Be part of our team."

I clicked on it one day, and within seconds an application form appeared. The form was hardly detailed, but I was sure it was because the Store would be doing their own investigative deep dive.

When they asked why we wanted to work there, we had planned the perfect answer: we were tired of the New York rat race. Tired of alternate side of the street parking, homeless beggars on every corner, squeezing four people into a crappy walk-up apartment built for two. We had a sincere desire to raise our kids in a proper community, with a real backyard, grass, trees…blah, blah, blah. We were writers. We knew that people outside New York loved anti–New York opinions, and even Megan, usually a very bad liar, followed my lead and fibbed like a pro. It worked.

Two days later I was having an online chat with a "marshal of human resources" who had the male-or-female name of Leslie. Leslie stated the Store's position unequivocally: *You're superqualified for marketing or business positions, but at the moment we can offer you employment in our beautiful new New Burg, Nebraska, fulfillment center.* I was aching to write the book. We were busting to be…well…spies. I was willing to take the job. So was Megan. We made a deal. And the Store made it clear that Megan and I were *not* being assigned to high-level, white-collar corporate jobs. No way. Ours were strictly factory jobs, filling orders and pasting on mailing labels. Yes, it was a truly shitty job. It required nothing more than a grammar-school education and a strong back.

Small computers would hang from chains around our necks. The computers would sputter out orders, and we would find the merchandise, collect it, and bring it to the packaging department (itself the size of a football stadium), then steer our little electronic go-karts back for another pickup. Only this time, instead of, say, a carton of Cap'n Crunch, a tube of hemorrhoid cream, a glass coffee table, and four copies of *Naked Hot Yoga at Home,* we might be fetching a chain for a John Deere hay baler, four jars of tangerine marmalade . . . you get the idea.

The add-ons were surprisingly seductive. The Store was supplying us with a three-bedroom house. They would also pay half the monthly mortgage of four hundred dollars. A fraction of what we'd been paying for our dingy apartment. We were sure that the Store must have made a mistake. But as we came to learn, the Store never makes mistakes.

Another e-mail said that our new house would be located in one of several Store-built communities. *Most of your neighbors will be employees of the Store.* Excellent: neighbors who might be possible sources for gossip and inside information.

It was starting to sound perfect. But of course, as spies, we were going to find the imperfections in that perfection. I'd be lying if I didn't say we were scared—two long-unemployed New York softies going to battle at one of the creepiest and fastest-growing companies in the United States.

But damn it, the book idea was too good to give up on.

CHAPTER 5

"MAN! THIS is soooo sweet!"

That was Alex's reaction when he first saw our new house at 400 Midshipman Lane, New Burg, Nebraska.

Frankly, we all had pretty much the same reaction.

It wasn't a mansion, but it was...well, man, soooo sweet. The kind of house that a midlevel tech executive might live in, not some guy who was packing toothpaste tubes and algebra textbooks into cardboard boxes. The house was white brick; it was long (very long) and low, with a three-car garage for our leased Acura.

The inside of the house was equally cool. Everything—from the ten-seat U-shaped charcoal-gray sofa in the living room to the crystal-and-bronze chandelier in the dining room—was LA trendy and top of the line. It was, as Megan pointed out, exactly how we would have decorated if we'd been able to afford it. Then we all took off in different directions to explore.

"Jacob, come in here. You gotta see this," Megan called from the kitchen.

By the time I joined her, she had already opened a large pantry cabinet.

"Yeah, okay," I said. "They told us in an e-mail they'd stock the place with some basics."

"Basics? Look. It's every brand we use. Not just Jif peanut butter and Frosted Flakes and Bumble Bee tuna but also Wilkin and Sons gooseberry conserve and Arrowhead Mills pancake mix."

A cabinet in the dining room contained Grey Goose vodka and J&B Scotch.

As we were studying the bar, Lindsay appeared at the dining-room door. She looked a bit confused.

"Look at this," she said. Then she held out the stuffed animal—Peabody the penguin—that she had owned since her first birthday.

"Hey, it's Peabody!" I said. "I thought you said you left him on the airplane."

"I did," Lindsay said. "But this is him. See? He has the tear on his collar and the chocolate stain on his chest. This is Peabody! He was waiting for me on the bed in my new room."

Lindsay looked nervous. I was about to examine the penguin more closely when I heard Alex's voice coming from the kitchen.

"Hey, Dad. There's a bunch of people at the back door."

CHAPTER 6

NOT JUST a bunch. A *big* bunch. Nine of them. Smiling, happy, good-looking men and smiling, happy, pretty women huddled around our back door like a sports team. They even seemed to have a captain—a very attractive woman in her early forties with shoulder-length brown hair and very tight jeans.

"I'm Marie DiManno," the woman said. "These are a few of your neighbors, and we're here to help you unpack."

I said exactly what I was thinking: "That's freaking amazing."

Megan clarified. "He means that's really very nice of you."

Marie added, "We saw the moving van outside, and we all texted each other. That's what friends are for."

I half expected them to launch into the song.

Fact is, we had been so engrossed by the penguin incident that we hadn't heard the moving van pull into the driveway. I looked over the heads of our neighbors and saw the movers. The four of them were dressed in navy-blue jumpsuits bearing the slogan THE MOVERS FROM THE STORE.

As the movers began carrying boxes into the house, Marie walked inside, told us to introduce ourselves to one another, and followed one of the movers up the front staircase.

We hit the receiving line—a group of people right out of central casting.

First we met the good-looking "older" couple. They were both trim and chic, with gray hair and elegant haircuts. They looked like a couple in one of those Cialis commercials.

Then a good-looking African American couple in their early forties, she in an impeccably faded denim shirt, both of them in light blue J.Crew Bermuda shorts.

Then the inevitable young, good-looking blond couple. The college quarterback and the college cheerleader.

And finally the all-purpose sitcom couple—the bald-headed guy with a potbelly and his wife with a wide mouth waiting to shoot out a wisecrack.

"I'm Mark Stanton," said the handsome black guy as he shook my hand. "Welcome to New Burg. This is my wife, Cookie."

Cookie said, "Welcome to the Store, and welcome to the Store *family*."

"That's a lot of welcoming," I said.

If they detected a note of sarcasm in my voice (and I had just meant to be funny, not sarcastic), their faces didn't register it.

I learned quickly that Mark Stanton worked in the fulfillment "gathering" building. (So that's what folks called the job—gathering. I'd be hearing that word a lot in the following hour or two.) It seemed that everyone who came out to help us worked in packing or shipping or gathering merchandise, except Marie. Marie was "resting" since the unexpected death of her husband. She had no "money-type concerns," she told me, "because the Store kindly provides a resting widow's pension."

The older gray-haired lady wasted no time telling me that "moving to New Burg and the Store will be the smartest thing you've ever done. Where else can you combine such nice work with such nice people in such a nice place? Martin and I had retired to Tampa, and frankly we were having trouble making ends meet. We have a son in Miami who's a drug addict."

She gave me this information as if she were telling us that her son was a dentist.

She continued. "Then Martin applied for a job at the Store. They hired us, shipped us out here just like you folks, and it's...well, it's made life worth living."

Our new neighbors appeared to be high-energy experts at unpacking. Marilyn Fidler, the pretty blond woman, had brought paper with which she proceeded to line the bedroom dresser drawers. (In a million years, Megan and I would not have thought to line our furniture drawers.)

"You want everything to start out as clean as possible," Marilyn said as she helped Megan and Lindsay fill two drawers with sweaters and sweatshirts.

As the busy morning wore on, Alex took me aside and

whispered, "Hey, Dad, you know what that Marie lady brought?"

"A great deal of energy," I said.

"No. She had this plasticky kind of shirt cardboard. She showed me how you fold T-shirts around it. She said it makes them stack up nice and neat, like on a store shelf. That's kind of creepy, no?"

"I don't know, buddy. I think she's just a perfectionist."

Alex looked doubtful, then he saw his sister carrying a box of *his* video games. He took off after her.

"Kind of creepy, no?" That's what Alex had said. I had disagreed with him, but I knew what he meant. Charming. Delightful. Friendly. Neat. Tidy. Industrious. Why were all those good things adding up to "creepy"?

Damn it, I thought. These folks are just being good neighbors.

And my son and I are just two typical cynical New Yorkers, too jaded to appreciate the simple life.

CHAPTER 7

NOT ONLY had I made Friday night's dinner, I was also such a cool husband that I was even doing the cleanup. Megan and the kids were outside exploring the backyard.

The meal itself had been a huge success: boeuf bourguignonne (Julia Child's secret recipe), Tuscan potato torta (Mario Batali's recipe), Key lime pie (Jacob Brandeis's recipe). Why Key lime pie? Whoever had stocked our kitchen included a graham cracker crust, sweetened condensed milk, eggs, and six perfect Key limes.

I was on my second Brillo pad when Megan returned to the kitchen.

"Jacob, c'mon outside," she said.

"Soon as I finish."

"No. Now. Right now." Her voice was surprisingly serious.

"Sure, sweetie," I said. But I wasn't moving fast enough for Megan.

"Now! Please. You've got to see this."

This time her voice was urgent. I didn't bother rinsing

my hands. I simply wiped off the pink Brillo suds with a dish towel.

"Look up there," Megan said, and she pointed (or so I thought) to the bright starry sky above the garage-door basketball hoop.

"It's a beautiful night," I said.

Impatience filled Megan's voice. "Show him, Alex."

Alex skipped a few feet to the hoop. He squatted, then he jumped and hung from the rim with his left hand. As Alex dangled he pointed to a small instrument made of glass and gray metal—almost undetectable against the gray paint of the garage. Then Alex snapped it from its holder. He dropped to the ground and tossed it to me.

"It's a camera," I said. "A tiny camera, like a...spy camera."

Megan, Lindsay, Alex, and I stared at it. We looked like a group who had just discovered a rare diamond. And I guess, in a way, we had.

I broke the silence.

"Son of a bitch!" I shouted. "In New York, they have street surveillance, but this shit is going too far. Cameras right in our own house."

"Jacob, calm down," Megan said.

"Megan! C'mon. People can expect reasonable god-damn privacy in their own houses, can't they?"

"Maybe in Nebraska the laws are different," Megan said.

"No," I said. I was beginning to shake with anger. "You can't ever do something like this in someone's house."

Then I exploded: *"That's illegal!"*

I looked at the tiny camera in my hand, then flung it with all my strength toward the garage door. I heard the crack, the immediate shattering of the pieces.

I rushed into the house. When a man goes beyond mad, he becomes a madman.

Megan and the kids were right behind me.

I looked around the kitchen. I began studying the ceiling and the tops of cabinets. In the tiny space between the Sub-Zero fridge and the appliance garage, where the industrial-size mixer was stored, was another camera. I wedged my fingers into the tiny space and pulled it out.

"*That's* illegal!" I yelled.

I found another camera in the window over the very sink where I'd been doing the dishes.

"*That's* illegal!" I yelled.

In the front hallway was a camera over the coat closet, perfect for recording guests.

"*That's* illegal!" I shouted.

Room to room. Lindsay was sobbing. Megan was as angry as I was.

Over the living-room fireplace.

"*That's* illegal!"

Behind the corner cabinet in the dining room.

"*That's* illegal!"

As I bounded up the stairs, Lindsay said, "They're probably watching you bust up their camera stuff."

"Let them. What the hell do I care? And you know why?" I yelled as I yanked a camera from the medicine cabinet in the kids' bathroom.

"Because *that's* illegal!"

From our bedroom to the attic. From the guest room to the playroom.

"Illegal! Illegal!"

We stood—a sweaty, crazed group of four—in the center of the playroom. The ghost of a video game made an occasional gargle on the TV screen. The silent furnace in the utility room cast a long shadow on the playroom floor. We surveyed the room. We were like the four-man crew of a ship that had survived a terrible storm.

"You think we got them all?" Megan asked.

The truthful answer would have been "No, I don't," but my wife and kids seemed scared enough.

I said, "Yeah, probably."

We sat at the bottom of the basement staircase. We were covered with perspiration. I was gasping for breath. There were a good sixty seconds of silence.

"What now?" Lindsay asked.

"Now we wait," I said. "It's their move."

CHAPTER 8

WE ALL slept badly.

I can't recall how many times Megan and I turned our heads and asked each other "Are you still awake?"

Or how many times I walked into Alex's room and said, "Either lower the music or use your earbuds."

No one was hungry for breakfast. Not even Alex, who's never been known to turn down food.

"How about we all take a drive and check out the downtown area?" I said.

I didn't expect anyone to agree to my suggestion. But Lindsay said, "Why not?" and Alex said, "I guess," and Megan gave a shrug that meant "Might as well." Okay, not an enthusiastic majority, but a majority nonetheless.

It was a quick drive from our house to downtown New Burg. No one brought up the surveillance cameras from the night before. Maybe we felt that if we didn't acknowledge it, then it didn't really happen. Or maybe we were just too spooked to dwell on it.

Ten minutes later we were standing at the corner of Brick Street and Mortar Street.

Alex gently punched Lindsay in the arm and mockingly said, "Brick and Mortar. Get it, dummy?"

"Of course I get it, you idiot," Lindsay said.

"Stop it, both of you," Megan said. "It's too hot to argue."

"Damn. It really is hot. Like a dry sauna," I said.

"Really different from New York," Alex said.

"No humidity," I said.

Not many other people were out walking. We all noticed *that*. Maybe it was the heat. Maybe.

We walked slowly. The combination of the intense heat and the perfect quaintness of the town was somehow hypnotizing. The town looked like an exquisitely built movie set—a movie from, say, the 1950s. A barbershop with a striped pole outside. A drugstore with a large brass apothecary scale in the window. A noble-looking First Bank of New Burg with what appeared to be real marble pillars at its entrance.

We walked silently, my eyes occasionally glancing up toward the street signs and the tops of small buildings in search of surveillance cameras. I was slowly becoming a man obsessed.

Something was strange about this downtown. We all felt it. But Megan was the first to put it into words.

"How many people do you see on the street?" she asked.

We looked around us.

"Fifteen," I said. "Not counting us."

"And how old do they look to you?" Megan asked.

We got it immediately. They were *all* old. Everyone was over seventy, some of them probably in their eighties. White-haired widows in pink-and-white pantsuits. Knobby-kneed old men in polyester shorts and imitation Lacoste shirts. One woman with a walker. One woman in a motorized wheelchair. A few old guys with canes.

"It all makes sense," I said. "That's why this downtown area exists—for the old people who just couldn't make the adjustment to the brave new world of the Store."

While drones hovered overhead, while the Store planned the techno-invasion of all consumer consumption, there remained a group of people who simply were not going to be part of it.

Clearly this downtown area had been created to soothe and seduce the elderly—people who did not want to use a Command key or an Option key. These were people who had to touch the oranges and smell the flowers and try on the shoes before they bought them. So the Store built a little town just for them. The Store knew it would be temporary; that sooner rather than later these old folks would die, and the world would be left to a new generation that could handle an iPad and a laptop and a cell phone at the same time.

We walked the wide wooden sidewalks. Inside the Drug Store, an elderly couple—he in baggy chinos, she in a very loose powder-blue caftan—sat at the counter. They each were drinking a chocolate malted. Behind the counter was a soda jerk from central casting—a bony young guy with rolled-up sleeves, a white apron, and a paper cap.

As we walked past the Jewelry Store, its window filled with charm bracelets and Timex watches, wedding bands and tiny diamond solitaire necklaces, two women passed us. Age guess? Both around seventy-five, both wearing billowing pants that looked like skirts (Megan later told me these items were called culottes). They both had very shiny silver hair and smiled when they saw us.

"Well, if it isn't the Brandeis family!" one of them said.

Before we could respond, the other woman announced our names as if she were a schoolteacher taking attendance.

"Megan, Jacob, Alex, and Lindsay."

"Yes, that's us," said Megan. "But how did you—"

"I meant to come by yesterday," the first woman said.

"I'll be over this week with a walnut streusel coffee cake, my specialty. So nice to meet you all," the second woman said, although they had never told us their names. Then they walked on briskly, still chuckling.

We four also kept walking. When we passed the Hardware Store, two very old men carrying cans of paint, folded tarps, and paint rollers tipped the visors on their baseball caps.

Almost in unison they said, "Welcome to New Burg, Mrs. Brandeis...Mr. Brandeis." Then they walked on.

We walked past a few more stores. The main street of town was almost ending. The last store sign said THE PIZZA STORE. Every shop had the word *store* in its name.

A drone was headed skyward, carrying a stack of four pizza boxes.

Then a big hulking blond guy walked out of the pizza

place carrying two pizza boxes. He was wearing cut-off jeans, a white T-shirt, and a baseball cap with the letter *N* imprinted on the front.

"Hey, man, watch the door," he said. His voice was deep and surly. He paused, then he broke into a big wide smile.

"Jacob, my man. I didn't realize it was you."

"It's all good," I said.

"I'm sorry, man. Is this the brood?"

"Uh, yeah. My family."

"Good to see you, gang. Jake's my man."

Then the big guy hit me gently on my shoulder and walked away.

Before anyone could ask, I said, "*No!* I have absolutely no idea who that guy was. But by the way, does anyone know what the *N* on his hat stands for?"

Lindsay had an answer.

"University of Nebraska?"

"No," I said. "It stands for *knowledge*."

All three of them groaned. I didn't even wait for the question Lindsay and Alex were about to ask. I simply said, "Listen. I don't know how they know our names. They just do. Maybe there's, like, a new arrivals section in the local paper. Maybe they all work for Welcome Wagon or saw our names on a church bulletin board."

Or maybe, I thought, *it could be something else.* I just didn't know what.

CHAPTER 9

"HEY, LOOK!" Alex said as he pointed across the street.

I hoped for something interesting, and I guess it was interesting—for him. Alex had spotted the Army and Navy Store.

"Let's check it out," I said.

So with no cars coming from either direction, we crossed the street. The kids crossed the street ahead of us and waited outside the store. As Megan and I stepped onto the sidewalk, we heard it before we saw it: a police car with a flashing light and siren.

A cop, fleshy and pink-faced, stepped out of the car. He was smiling ever so slightly.

"Mr. Brandeis, isn't it?" the cop said. Like everyone else in New Burg, he was determined to be impeccably polite.

"Uh...yeah," I said.

He looked at Megan, tipped an imaginary hat toward her, and said, "Good morning to you, too, Mrs. Brandeis."

"Good morning," Megan said softly.

"Do you folks realize you just broke the law?"

"We did?" Megan said.

"Jaywalking is against the law here," the officer said. I wanted to say, "You've got to be kidding," but the cop, though polite, was also deadly serious.

"Well, there were no cars. So we thought..." I realized that I was foolish to say anything.

"Mr. Brandeis, a law is a law. A rule is a rule."

I nodded. But the officer wasn't finished talking.

"Jaywalking. *That's* illegal."

Megan and I looked at each other. I saw the fear in her eyes.

"Maybe in New York City they flaunt the law," he said. (I thought this would be a bad time to tell him that the correct verb was *flout,* not *flaunt.*)

He went on. "But here in New Burg, if you don't follow the rules, well... *that's* illegal."

"But... we..."

"No problem, Mr. Brandeis. Let's just call this conversation... a warning?"

He tipped his imaginary hat once again.

"Welcome to New Burg," he said, and he got back in the patrol car and sped off.

We stood silently for a few seconds. We pretended we were looking at the bomber jackets and khaki cargo pants in the store window.

Then my daughter turned and put her arms around me. She hugged me tightly, and I could feel her tears against my chest. It was her brother, however, who spoke next.

"We're scared, Dad. This isn't fun. This is no fun at all."

They were too old for the usual parental bullshit. I couldn't say, "Oh, c'mon, there's nothing to be scared about." I couldn't say, "Whaddya mean 'no fun'? What about the goofball guy with the baseball cap? This crazy old cop was like something from a movie. Nothing to be scared of."

Instead I said, "I know how you feel. I'm scared, too."

Alex put his arms around my side. Megan moved toward me and touched my face. Then Megan spoke.

"Of course we're all scared."

My wife, ladies and gentlemen. Now, there's one smart and wonderful woman.

CHAPTER 10

MEGAN AND I were absolute suckers for old bookstores and old libraries. So when we saw the words NEW BURG FREE LIBRARY engraved on a sign in front of a small red-brick building, we smiled knowingly at each other and headed to the library's white front door.

The library was open. We walked in.

An old-fashioned feather duster sat on the tall wooden checkout desk. But apparently the duster had not been used in quite a while; a thin layer of dust covered just about every surface.

I counted ten rows of dark wood shelves. A random survey of the library collection indicated that there was nothing much that had been published after the 1930s. I saw a lot of Sinclair Lewis—*Babbitt, Main Street, Dodsworth.* I saw a few old bestsellers—*Grand Hotel, Back Street, Saratoga Trunk.* Megan pointed out a big selection of Agatha Christie and a small selection of William Faulkner. But none of the books seemed to have ever been opened. When I took down a copy of *Gone with the Wind,* the spine of the book cracked gently; the pages were pristine.

"Megan! Jacob!" A crisp, stern woman's voice shot through the room.

The voice rang out again: "I'm in the home crafts and culinary section. Don't move. I know where you are."

So we did not move. I just turned to Megan and said, "Oh, shit: we're probably in trouble again."

Walking around the end of the fiction section was a woman about forty years old. Her hair was pulled back. She wore a simple gray linen smock, and her face was so plain that I could not tell if she was smiling or scowling.

"I'm Deb Borelli. I'm the librarian."

"And you seem to know who we are," Megan said.

"Everybody knows everybody in New Burg," she said. Maybe there was the start of a smile on her face.

"I see," I said. As if what she had said was actually an explanation.

"May I answer any questions you might have?"

I had a thousand questions. Why was the library empty? Why was the library dirty? Why were there no books less than seventy-five years old? Why does everybody recognize us and know our names? Why are only old people walking the downtown streets?

"No. I don't have any questions, but thank you," Megan said. "Jacob? Any questions for Ms. Borelli?"

"Oh, please," the librarian said. "I hate the word *Ms*. It tells you absolutely nothing about a woman."

I wanted to say, "Well, that's the whole point," but I

was learning to keep my smart mouth shut in New Burg. Megan was much better about it than I was.

"So is it Miss or Mrs.?" Megan asked.

Now the librarian smiled. It was gracious. I was certain that it was also phony.

"Not Miss. It's Mrs."

"Oh, you're married?" Megan said.

"Yes, I'm married."

Ever the charmer, I said, "Well, no doubt we'll meet Mr. Borelli one of these days."

The librarian spoke.

"No. You won't."

Uh-oh—a divorce or a death. I stepped in it again.

"My husband's been transferred," she said.

There was a silence. Deb Borelli's face was vacant. Her eyes looked back and forth between Megan and me. I decided to say something.

"Transferred. What exactly does that mean?"

Her eyes narrowed. Her chin quivered a tiny bit. Then she spoke.

"He's...been transferred."

Never content to make a small mistake, I then turned it into a big mistake.

"What do you mean by 'transferred'?" I said.

"What I mean is: he's not here anymore."

She turned quickly and began to walk away. "You'll have to excuse me now."

CHAPTER 11

WE WERE tired and angry and nervous when we returned to our car. So as I drove we did what every normal American family does: we argued like idiots and got on one another's nerves.

"Why don't *you* sit in the back for a change, Mom?" Alex said. He had a definite snarkiness in his voice. And I really was not in the mood for it.

"Your mother always sits in the front," I said. "That's the rule. So don't start."

"That time we drove to Albany she didn't sit in the front," he said.

Lindsay joined the action.

"That's because you acted like a baby and lied. You said you were getting carsick when you weren't. You've never gotten carsick in your life."

"I get carsick whenever I look at you," Alex answered.

Suddenly (and unexpectedly) Megan exploded.

"Stop it. Both of you. Just stop it. Only imbeciles would argue about where we should sit in the goddamn car."

To ward off a potential escalation, I said, "And don't either of you make a joke or an insult about 'only imbeciles.'"

Before I or anyone else could say anything, I saw a flashing light in the rearview mirror. It was accompanied by a siren.

"What the hell is that for?" I said. Then, almost reflexively, I pulled onto the shoulder of the road. I shifted the car into Park, and I rechecked the rearview mirror.

Oh, it was definitely a police car, and the red light was still flashing.

Alex and Lindsay were taking turns shouting, "What's happening?" and "What's going on?"

"Don't turn around!" I yelled, and I really had no idea why I said that. I squinted hard, alternating my gaze between the rearview and the side-view mirror.

I could not be certain, but I suspected that the round face and wide shoulders I saw in the mirrors belonged to the same cop who gave us the scary-stern warning for jaywalking.

Why wasn't he getting out of his police car?

The light kept whirling. Then another siren. This one from another car, a different police car. Now this new car pulled in front of my own stopped car. Then the siren stopped. I wasn't sure whether I was supposed to get out of my car...yet I was vaguely recalling that you're supposed to stay *in* your car...on the other hand, if I didn't get out I might piss off the cops. Suddenly a blast of sound erupted from the loudspeaker on the patrol car behind me.

Police info for halted vehicle. Police info for
halted vehicle.

Please proceed to place of residence. Repeat. Please proceed to place of residence.
Maintain legal speed limit. Proceed now.

"What are we going to do now, Dad?" Alex asked.

At that moment I was feeling virtually every feeling
a man could feel. I felt furious, stupid, embarrassed. I
hooked on furious, of course, and I fired back at my
son.

"Are you deaf? The guy couldn't have been clearer.
We're supposed to drive home. You know, our goddamn
place of residence. You heard him as well as I did."

There was a creeping numbness in my arms and
hands. But I managed to pull out into the very light
traffic. As I did, the police car in front of me anticipated
the move. He, too, pulled out, staying in front of me. I
couldn't pass the legal speed limit even if I wanted to.

Yet in all the chaos and confusion I was suddenly
aware that Megan had remained very quiet.

"Whaddya think?" I said softly.

"I think we should do what they ask," she said, equally
softly.

Then from the backseat, Lindsay spoke: "Any ideas,
Daddy?"

"No," I said.

"Nothing?" Alex asked.

They seemed just short of stunned that the dad with
all the answers—"You work with your knees for a jump

shot"; "A little more reading and a little less computer wouldn't kill you"—had absolutely no answer.

In almost no time—no time at all—it seemed that we were turning into our driveway. I glanced up at the surveillance cameras, still there. I saw a neighbor trimming the bushes under her dining-room window.

The cop cars stopped in front of and behind me.

I was uncertain whether or not my family and I should exit the car. Then the front patrol car made a U-turn and left the driveway. The one behind me remained.

I was expecting something bad. The police officer behind me stepped out of his car. He walked toward my car. He motioned us to exit. I unlocked the doors. We stepped out.

Yes, it was indeed the same pink-faced asshole who had stopped us for jaywalking, who lectured us and frightened us and pretty much humiliated us.

"So there you are," the officer said with a big fat smile on his big fat face. "The Brandeis family got a fancy police escort home. The New Burg police wanted to prove that we can be your enemy . . . or we can be your friend."

He gave us an informal two-finger salute and walked back to his car. He opened the car door. Just before he got in he spoke.

"You all have a nice day, now."

CHAPTER 12

THAT SATURDAY night, after a drone had delivered a delicious dinner of veal parmigiana, arugula salad, and pizza margherita from the Pizza Store (we were quickly embracing the various conveniences of living in the world of the Store), Megan and I settled into our "office" in the attic— a tiny corner space where we had decided to write our tell-all book.

People told us the dry heat of the Midwest would be a relief after the humid heat of Manhattan. They lied. Our attic was scorching. The central air-conditioning didn't reach that far up, and the fan served mainly to toss around our index cards and printer paper.

We had chosen the attic in case there were still some cameras we may have missed in other rooms. Yes, a few spycams were most likely hidden in the attic (we're not *that* naive), but after we removed two that were attached to wooden roof beams we thought we had a good shot at privacy.

But who the hell knew with these people?

One lightbulb dangled over the small card table we were using as a desk. The heat was so intense that we had stripped down to our underwear. The ice cubes melted in our iced coffees.

Most of the house felt like it had been built the previous week, but the attic looked like it was two hundred years old: cobwebs and rodent droppings on most of the beams, creaking floorboards, and, in the stifling heat, something we couldn't explain—an occasional shot of very cold air.

More troubling than that, however, was the question Megan asked before we had written a single word of our book.

"How did this happen, Jacob? How did we end up sitting half naked in a hundred-and-ten-degree attic in Nebraska writing a book about some insane company?"

It was a good question, one that I had also been pondering. Unfortunately I didn't have the remotest idea of a good response.

"Maybe we're just destined to write this book," I said.

"Not to be cynical, sweetie, but that's way too strange an answer—like God wants us to write the book."

"Not God," I said. "But I don't know. Maybe fate."

"'Fate' is just shorthand for 'God.'"

"I guess," I said. "But it does seem that everything just kind of came together—the rap book being turned down, our becoming really aware of the Store, then our needing the job and the money. It's like we enlisted in the army for a war, kind of a *holy* war."

"I guess," she said, but it was clear that we were both

a little scared. She went on. "If we get caught, we'll be ... well, I can't even imagine what they could do to us."

"Ugga-bugga," I said.

"Ugga-bugga is right," Megan answered. No smile. Yes, we definitely were scared. Then she said, "Why don't we just get to work?"

And so we did. Both Megan and I used the same system when we were writing nonfiction. We wrote everything, every little piece of fact or opinion or interview quotation, on index cards. We filed them and sorted them and filed them again. We kept small files of cards as sub-files of large files. Eventually we would have thousands of cards, stored carefully and sorted precisely, in hundreds of plastic boxes (which, of course, we bought from a stationery supplier on the Store's website).

Although, like most people our age, we lived our lives excessively on our laptops, we could not find a satisfying way to put our nonfiction research on the computer. We somehow needed to see the shoe boxes, to riffle through them, to move the index cards and Post-it notes around as new information came into the work.

Oh, we still used the Internet a lot.

The original Indian name of New Burg, Nebraska? Go to Google. (The name, by the way, is an anglicized form of *nom-bah,* the Quapaw word for the number 2.)

Do consumers believe there is a significant difference between items bought online and those purchased in brick-and-mortar stores? Hello, Google. (Turns out that most people don't care.)

That night, however, we were mainly in index-card

territory. A number of cards were written about Deb the librarian and her husband, who had been "transferred." There were about ten cards about the guy coming out of the Pizza Store. Brick Street meeting Mortar Street. The surveillance-camera search. The neighbors who came to help. The cop and his kind "warning." On and on and on.

Our number 2 pencils scratched away, interrupted only by an unexpected whoosh of icy air.

Our shoulders seemed to start aching at about the same time. We arched our backs. We stretched our arms.

Then Megan said, "When did they deliver that box over there?"

I looked around. She pointed to a box marked THE STORE HOME OFFICE SUPPLIES.

"I have no idea," I said. "Is it stuff you ordered?"

"No. I haven't ordered a thing since we got to New Burg."

We walked the few yards to the box. It was snuggled under a wooden slope in the roof. We opened it easily enough and looked inside: two cellophane-wrapped packages of number 2 pencils, fifteen packets of index cards in various sizes and colors, a small cardboard box containing ten Rolling Writer pens, and, weirdest of all, two thick memo pads. One said FROM THE DESK OF MEGAN BRANDEIS. The other was identical except, of course, it had my name at the top.

"Are you sure *you* didn't order these?" Megan asked. "I mean, Jesus, it's exactly the stuff we use."

"Yeah, like the peanut butter and the cereal they had for us." Both of us simply did not want to discuss it.

It was almost 2:00 a.m. And it was clearly time to call it a night.

"Somehow I feel about ten times more awake than I did when we started," Megan said.

"Good. Let's not waste the energy," I said. "Pull up the Store site."

Megan threw me a what-are-you-up-to look, but the site came up, and the page read as it always did:

Welcome to the Store
It's All You Need in Life

I took the laptop from her, and Megan watched over my shoulder as I tapped away.

I went to "The Store for Books." This is how the Store had begun its merchandising conquest of the world—selling books. They maintained the largest collection of books in the world, bigger than the collection at the Library of Congress. Classics, bestsellers, textbooks, kids' books, porn—everything you could imagine putting between two covers.

In addition to all those traditional books was a unique section: "Request a Book You'd Like to See Written." This section of the Store website was filled with title suggestions for books that didn't yet exist—*How to Spay Your Pet at Home* (I swear) and *The Tao of Algorithms* were two of many thousands.

I moved to the subsection headlined with the letter *U*. There, right after the title *The Ultimate Book of Zen Orchestral Accompaniment*, I clicked on "Submit your book request."

I carefully typed in *"Ulysses: The Perfect Sleep Aid."*

The following sentence filled the screen: "We'll get to your request as soon as possible. Check back frequently."

I looked at Megan, who was laughing. Then we kissed.

The kiss was filled with a mixture of love and sex and fear.

"I hope they have a sense of humor," Megan said.

"We'll soon find out."

"Yeah," said Megan. "We'll check back frequently."

"But for now, let's beat it," I said.

"Yes, let's. I'm getting really cold," Megan said.

I looked at my computer screen. It read: TIME: 2:14 A.M. TEMP: 45 F.

CHAPTER 13

"HEY, IT'S Sunday," I said. "Let's all go to church."

From the astonished expressions on my family's faces and the long silence that followed, I might as well have said, "Let's all go to Mars."

Alex spoke first. "What's up with you, Dad? Are you, like, trying out a stand-up comedy routine?"

I didn't respond, but fifteen minutes later, the kids having opted to stay home, Megan and I—she in a yellow dress printed with white daisies, I in a blue linen blazer—were driving toward the *only* church in New Burg for the eleven o'clock service.

The two of us were not particularly religious. As a couple, the last time we had been in a house of worship was eighteen years earlier, when we got married at the Larchmont Temple. Then we were in a holy place because of love. This time we were going for research.

The church was called the New Burg Church of God, a perfectly okay name but without a touch of creativity to it. You know, like Catholic churches called the Most

Precious Blood of Jesus or Our Lady, Sorrowful Star of the Sea. Same with temples whose names always sounded like my grandmother's Yiddish expressions: Anshe Emeth Shalom or Temple Shaaray Tefila.

At 10:55 the church parking lot was packed. Whatever they were selling at the New Burg Church of God, the people of New Burg were certainly buying it. Latecomers like us, arriving only a few minutes before curtain time, had to park at the far end of the lot.

We got out of the car and instinctively tugged at our clothes and patted our hair. Megan and I were strangers in a strange land.

Then we heard a voice.

"Don't worry. You both look just fine."

It was a man's voice—slow, deep, and slightly slurred—and it was coming from the passenger side of a car parked directly next to ours. Megan and I flashed embarrassed smiles, and I said something inane: "Thank you very much. So do you."

"Well, frankly, we don't. See for yourself," said the man.

He opened the car door, stood up, and stretched himself out to about six feet tall. He was dark-skinned, maybe East Indian, maybe Mediterranean. His hair was sloppy, and his sport shirt was wrinkled, but he was also handsome. He had that I-just-swam-in-the-ocean look that a lot of women seem to like.

His female companion moved out from the driver's side. She was pretty hot. She was almost as tall as he was, with long blond hair. Both of them looked about our age.

Something else got out of the car with them—the thick, sweet, beautiful scent of marijuana smoke. I know there's no such thing as a contact high, but if I were ever going to get one, that would have been the time. Our parking-lot neighbors must have been smoking with the car windows rolled up, because the smell of weed was moving toward us like a tiny cyclone.

"My name is Bud, Bud Robinson, and the slightly stoned blonde over there is my wife, Bette—that's Bette with an *e*, not a *y*—and you *do* pronounce the *e*."

I was still processing the spelling and pronunciation of Bette's name when I saw Bud looking at his cell phone. He began reading aloud.

"And you two are Megan and Jacob Brandeis. Jacob, a former writer and an NYU grad. Megan, also a former writer and—woo-hoo—a Stanford grad."

Bette was exhaling from a long hit on the joint they were sharing. Then she spoke. "It's all kinda creepy, isn't it?"

Bud built on her question: "Ya know, how everybody knows everything about everyone else. That's the Store for you."

"Is it all because of the Store?" Megan asked.

We were both being cautious.

The response to Megan's question was a burst of laughter from Bette and Bud. My translation of their laughter was: "Are you two so simple that you couldn't figure that out for yourselves?"

Bette had passed the joint to Bud. He had taken a hit. Then he offered it to Megan.

Megan took it, took a small puff, then handed the joint to me. It was pretty clear that we were going to be late for church.

Bud rubbed his head and spoke.

"Now, the other thing it says on my old handheld here is that you live at 400 Midshipman Lane. *We* live at 420 Midshipman."

"I guess that makes you the only people in the neighborhood who didn't come and help us unpack," Megan said.

"We were preoccupied with recreation, if you know what I mean," Bud said, and he tipped his head toward the new joint he was rolling.

Then Bette said, "I'm just curious. I like asking all the newcomers this question."

"Shoot," I said.

"Have you found the surveillance cameras yet?"

"Well, uh...yeah," I said. Then Megan added, "The first night here."

"I've got some advice for you," Bud said. "Don't even bother trying to remove those cameras."

"Too late," I said.

"The Store'll just sneak them back in. They've probably got a robot drone in your house right now, messing around with all new cameras."

Bud inhaled the weed deeply, and he let it out slowly.

"You folks going into the church service?" he asked.

"I guess we should. Better late—" I said.

"You don't have to go in," Bette said. She then explained that last year they learned that the surveillance cameras took attendance by recording the cars entering the parking lot, not by recording the people actually entering the church.

"Are you sure of that?" I asked.

"Not really," Bette said. "With the Store you can never be absolutely sure of anything."

I realized that I was liking these people. This cool guy and his hot wife. Yet I was afraid to like them too much.

I don't think Bette could read my mind, but she sure could read the situation. Suddenly but calmly she said, "I bet you two are thinking, 'We just met these people. Can we trust them?'"

Megan and I smiled. Nervously.

Then I said, "Well, can we? Can we trust you?"

Bud's voice was full of hearty laughter as he spoke.

"Of course not! Are you crazy? We work for the Store."

CHAPTER 14

MONDAY MORNING Megan and I went to work. At the Store fulfillment center.

Eighteen buildings covering three square miles. Eighteen buildings connected by causeways and tunnels and bridges and trams with miles of escalators and conveyor belts in between. Drones flew above the buildings, and humans in navy-blue jumpsuits worked within them.

NO WORRIES

That was the sign that hung on the walls, on the backs of chairs, on the free soda machines, the free snack machines, the free coffee-cappuccino-espresso machines.

NO WORRIES

That was the sign that hung over the thousands of video monitors, over the entrances and exits, even over the urinals in the men's rooms.

Of course Megan and I had nothing *but* worries. Would we be caught taking notes? Would we be found out?

We had just joined thousands of workers. Hundreds of those workers said, "Welcome, friends" as we were escorted by a smiling young woman to the fulfillment center's underground garage. It was in that massive garage that we saw our first Stormer, a computer-controlled driverless vehicle.

If a golf cart and a Porsche had given birth, their offspring would be a Stormer, an efficient merchandise-gathering machine that plied the lanes of the fulfillment-center buildings. Gatherers like Megan and me jumped on and off to gather what everyone at the Store called the stuff.

It seemed that every kind of "stuff" in the world was in those eighteen enormous buildings. Approximate size? Imagine fifteen Madison Square Gardens.

Did you need a leather three-piece sectional sofa, a watermelon and a melon baller, a Patek Philippe watch, an ironing board, two thousand plastic-recycling bags, red paper clips, or an autographed Mickey Mantle baseball card? Maybe you'd like a low-flush toilet, a package of condoms, a Roku box, a pasta machine, a fifty-thousand-dollar Edwardian diamond tiara, a pound of sevruga caviar, a thousand pounds of manure, a napkin holder, a *case* of napkin holders, a Hershey's Special Dark chocolate bar, a *case* of Hershey's Special Dark chocolate bars, a canoe, a Jet Ski, a box of colostomy bags, a...

If it existed, the Store sold it. The Stormers zoomed around like roaches running from the light. The workers popped up and down like characters in old silent movies.

Megan and I watched it all as our Stormer took us on a "training and orientation" tour. A woman's soothing voice came through our earbuds as we rode along:

"At the moment, you're witnessing the assembly of a packing crate. Watch the merchandise being lifted into the crate. The follow-up accountant checks the order and..."

Every few yards, the voice would resume: "At the moment we're in 'semiperishables,' everything from jicama and avocados to deviled eggs and smoked salmon. The temperature in this area is precisely calibrated to..."

Then a surprise.

We were making a left turn from "photo printing and three-dimensional laser printing" to "all-natural flooring, door saddles, and colonial molding" when a hand reached toward my head and pulled off my earbuds.

The assailant, whom I hadn't yet identified, spoke in a loud stage whisper: "Welcome to Planet Crazy. Please check your brain at the entrance."

It was Bud.

"Holy shit!" I said.

"Watch your mouth, New York boy," I heard a woman say. It was Bette.

Yes, our two pothead friends from the church parking lot.

Bette showed us the face of her standard-issue Store tablet as she said, "We tracked your orientation path on the 'Who's New' page. Take a gander."

On Bette's tablet were two very retouched photos of Megan and me. We looked like models in a 1950s clothing catalog. The caption below our picture read "Say hello to Meg and Jake."

Meg? Jake?

Megan shook her head and said, "And so the madness begins."

"And it *is* only the beginning," Bud said.

"We've got to scoot," said Bette. "We can talk later. We'll stop by soon."

Bette and Bud walked away quickly. And Megan and I slipped our earbuds back in.

The voice of the guide began again, "Now that your *unscheduled visit* is ended . . ."

Someone had been watching us.

The voice continued, "Please report to assignment area 44 for your first task." The voice clicked off.

The Stormer made a sudden sharp right turn at "smoke detectors, fire extinguishers, and carbon monoxide detectors."

In approximately ten minutes we had arrived at assignment area 44. During that ten-minute drive I had counted ninety-five Store slogan signs.

NO WORRIES

No worries?

In my opinion, nothing *but* worries.

CHAPTER 15

AT THE Store assignment area a bell rang, and a text message appeared on our tablet.

The success of the Store depends on the excitement and involvement of the consumers we serve. Sometimes our friends the consumers are so pleased with the low price and easy delivery of the goods they buy that they become totally immersed. When that happens, our friends at home need some help and guidance from their friends at the Store.

Today, Meg and Jake, you two, as a team, will be representing us as we try to help folks break away from their commitment to the products they're using. In other words, let's get them out of their houses and return them to service. Many of them have been on extended leaves of absence.

Please review the prepared talking points as your Stormer takes you to your first stop. Good luck.

So a Stormer took us to visit Store customers who had become "so engrossed" in Store merchandise that they needed to be "deimmersed and reimmersed." The objective was to get people to stop using their favorite Store products and go back to work.

Our first stop was a big Tudor-style house. According to the information on our tablets, the thirty-year-old couple living there had not left the place for sixty-five days. That's right, sixty-five days. They had become obsessed with using their small army of Vitamix blenders.

"Man, take one sweet sip of the red cabbage, kale, and blueberry," the husband said at his doorway, holding out a big glass of very unappetizing blue-tinged mud.

"No, thank you," I said.

"Ma'am," he said, offering the same potion to Megan.

I don't think the guy had shaved in sixty-five days. He was wearing a dingy T-shirt and red boxer shorts, both covered with stains the same color as the juice he was offering.

"We're two of your friends from the Store," Megan said.

"And you are friends indeed." It was a different voice, a woman's voice.

Then we saw the woman. She easily weighed 250 pounds.

"Our friends at the Store sold us our Vitamix machines, and those mixers or blenders or whatever they are have just changed our lives."

She, too, held a big glass of liquid. She called her offering a chocolate yogurt ambrosia smoothie.

"Tastes delicious, and it's good for what ails you," she said.

I took the glass. I took a gulp. It was exceptionally delicious. It was also exceptionally sweet and exceptionally rich. I would have bet that she'd been drinking gallons of similar smoothies for the previous sixty-five days.

Megan and I tried to tempt them with the benefits of "getting back to your colleagues at the Store." Their reaction? They invited us into the kitchen to see their "family."

The family consisted of five different Vitamix machines: two CIA Professional Series blenders, two Professional Series 500 blenders, and a G-series 780.

"The G-series is the next generation," the wife whispered confidentially.

They described their lives—if you could call what they were doing living.

The husband ordered his juicing produce—from leeks to oranges to avocados—from the Store. The wife ordered her Chobani yogurt and Mast Brothers chocolate from the Store.

The husband said it perfectly: "The Store makes everything so easy that you never have to leave your house." He paused for a moment and then added, "Well, sometimes you do, but just once. I was playing Pokémon GO." Then he laughed.

They elaborated on this theme. This couple subscribed to the Store's streaming services for movies and TV and sports specials. The Store filled their medical prescriptions ("I have a touch of diabetes, so I gotta have my metformin," the wife said). The Store sold them "a really reasonably priced" Thermador refrigerator in which to keep their overflow of smoothies. The drones delivered their food.

"But what about people, human contact, your friends?" Megan asked.

"Who needs them when you have this?" the woman said.

We left.

Our next stop was only two houses away from the Vitamix couple.

The door was unlocked. So we walked into a big front hall filled with mirrors, clouds of hot steam, and the scent of eucalyptus and menthol. The sounds of exotic music—harp and piano and waterfall—filled the air.

A woman entered, perhaps fifty years old, wearing a long white terry-cloth bathrobe. Her blond hair looked wet; it was pulled back. She asked sweetly if she could help us.

Before I could answer, Megan said, "Wow. You've got some kind of luxury spa in here."

The blond woman spoke: "We think it *is* a luxury spa in here."

She was immediately joined by a smaller version of herself—a thirtyish blond woman, also in a white terry-cloth robe. They had to be mother and daughter.

"I bet you folks are from the Store, aren't you?" the younger woman asked.

We said we were.

"It won't work," the older woman said. "You two aren't the first. They've sent plenty of others. Over the past six months there must have been ten different people from the Store. Sometimes couples, most times women. But the thing is this: they see what we've done with the place, and sometimes they don't want to leave, either. The massage machines, the saunas, even the three attendants . . . we call 'em the boys. We got them all from the Store, and now the Store says we should get back to work. Well, why should we? They keep extending our paid leave. And . . . why should we leave all this?"

I suggested that returning to a life of accomplishment and people—the joking, the parties—would be fun.

They laughed at me. They thought I was crazy.

"We have air purifiers, tanning beds, everything we need," the younger woman said.

Then they took us on a short tour of their magical mystery spa, and it was . . . well, it was a real spa. Another young blond woman was being massaged by a well-built older man. A fat hairy guy sat in a dry sauna. A very old woman sat in a wet sauna.

"Is this a legit business here?" I asked.

"Oh, no," said the older woman. "Just friends and family."

Unsuccessful again. We left the spa. Megan said, "I feel like a Jehovah's Witness."

"What do you mean?"

"Door-to-door but no converts."

Back in the Stormer I gave her a short, sweet kiss. "Ugga-bugga," I said.

"No," Megan said. "The proper expression is . . ."

She paused for a few moments, and then, almost in unison, we said, "No worries."

CHAPTER 16

THE NEXT day Megan and I were separated...at work. In our strange new world this was a strange new feeling—being alone. Megan and I were always together, especially during the previous few months: working on the disastrous *Roots of Rap,* organizing the move to New Burg, moving in, working in the attic on the new project. Now we were alone, which was unusual for us.

We were each assigned our own Stormer, working in different buildings. That second day I was assigned to "collection housewares," gathering and prepacking wall-mounted plastic-bag dispensers, silicone spatulas, apple-pie-scented candles, and disposable espresso cups.

Megan was assigned to "maternity denim," filling orders for elastic-waist butt-lifting black jeans, stretch-sided white twill jeans, and elastic-waist distressed jeans with "worn, torn, not yet born" holes at the knees.

We drove back home together, of course. Megan did the driving, and I did the writing, filling index cards with notes ("Quick calculation: free cafeteria lunches cost the Store approximately $830,000 daily") and observations ("Pretty sure the 'collection housewares' supervisor has small computer chip embedded in his forearm"), and personal insights ("Stormer check-in staff all nice, polite; Stormer repairmen all suck").

When we arrived home our plan was to check in with Alex and Lindsay, then use the matching treadmills in the basement for half an hour, do fifteen minutes on the StairMaster, and finally cool down with a few icy Sam Adamses.

As I say, that was our plan. Alex was waiting at the open garage door.

No "Hello." No "How was your day?"

His greeting was, "Do you know two people named Bette and Bud?"

"Yes," said Megan, and then, quite sanctimoniously, she added, "We met them at church."

First Alex said, "Alleluia." Then he said, "Well, they're in the dining room, and they just droned in a bucket of Buffalo wings and fries."

We walked into the dining room and were greeted by lots of hugs. Bette and Bud obviously subscribed to the hugging craze that was sweeping the country, including New Burg.

"I warned you we'd be coming by," said Bette.

We told them how pleased we were that they just dropped in, that we had absolutely nothing planned for the evening, and that Buffalo wings were some of our favorite foods in the world.

They didn't seem nearly as hip and good-looking as

the previous two times we'd met. Bette seemed pale and wasn't wearing makeup. Her clothes were loose and matronly, and she wore a foolish-looking pink sweatshirt. Bud had a puffiness around the eyes. He was wearing "Dad" pants—baggy, pleated chinos belted high on his stomach.

"Took us exactly two minutes to walk here," Bud said. "Door to door; timed it."

Bette said, "Can you *think* of anything more boring than to use a stopwatch on a walk down the block? Next he'll be counting raindrops."

"By the way," Bud said. "It looks like we were right about something."

"About what?" I asked.

Bud tilted his head in the direction of the fireplace. "The spaniels," he said.

Both Megan and I turned our heads toward the mantel and the early nineteenth-century ceramic cocker spaniels Megan's grandmother had given us.

I must have looked confused.

"He's talking about this," Bette said. She walked to the fireplace, picked up one of the dogs, and turned it upside down. You didn't have to be a CIA operative to spot the surveillance camera that had been drilled into the dog's paw.

"Son of a bitch," I said.

"Please, Jacob," Megan said. "Don't start."

I surveyed the living room and front hall. Yes, the cameras were back, reinstalled, just as Bette and Bud had predicted. Over the front door. Over the hall mirror. Over the hall closet. Over the fake Matisse in the living room. In some of the same places. And in a bunch of new ones. "Get used to it, man," Bud said. "This is the way the Store works. And there isn't anything you can do about it."

He paused. He smiled. Then he said, "Nothing but this..."

Bud leaped up and began singing the teenybop song of the hour, "Jealous." He held the camera-loaded china dog as if it were a microphone. As Bud sang and gyrated and did a third-rate imitation of Nick Jonas, moving the dog back and forth in front of his face, Megan and I were a little bit too stunned to laugh. Man, the guy was moving with passion.

I don't like the way he's lookin' at you.

He stopped suddenly. He plopped back down.

"I always like to provide a little entertainment for the bastards who have to watch all these videos. You should see my Lady Gaga. It's perfect."

Bette then said, "Of course, you should know that since Bud's wacko performance was recorded on one of the cameras in *your* house, the Store will bring it up in your interview."

"We're being interviewed?" Megan asked.

"Sure thing. Everyone who moves here has a three-hour introductory interview. They call it the in-in. You bring the whole family. The kids. Even a dog or a canary if you've got one. Then they ask about a zillion questions. Some highly personal. Some highly intellectual. And some just plain crazy."

"They're very polite, very courteous," said Bud. "No one seems to know what they do with the results," he said. "But it's nothing to worry about."

From the looks on their faces, we knew it was nothing to look forward to, either.

CHAPTER 17

THE VERY next day Megan, Lindsay, Alex, and I were seated in a large comfortable room.

"Lindsay, let's start with you. Name two things you'd change about your parents if you could."

The walls were paneled in dark wood. The furniture was classic psychiatrist-office stuff: Eames chair, brown-and-black tweed sofa, matching tweed club chair, and, of course, a coffee table topped with a box of Kleenex.

"Jacob, would you ever skip church on Sunday to go to a Major League Baseball game?"

The interviewer was named Justin—a skinny guy with the standard good looks of a TV game-show host. No idea whether he was a real psychiatrist.

"Megan, are you an organ donor?"

Justin said that this was a purely get-to-know-you session. They did it with all new employees and their families.

Justin told us something he would repeat a number of times throughout our three hours there. "There are no right or wrong answers." Yeah, sure.

"Lindsay, what do you miss most about New York City?"

"The craziness."

"Megan, do you believe that thirteen is an unlucky number?"

Megan said she was not a superstitious person.

"Follow-up, then. Would you live in an apartment on the thirteenth floor?"

"Well, like I said, I'm not superstitious. So I guess I would."

"Another follow-up. You said 'I guess I would.' Does that mean you're not certain?"

Megan said she was certain.

"Alex, same question. Thirteenth floor?"

Alex was ready: "I tend to live wherever my parents live."

"Good answer, my man."

Justin had no paper or pen. He took no notes. I could only assume that we were being recorded or even streamed on video. Had he conducted these interviews so many times that he had it all memorized? Did he just invent things as he went along? Or was it a combination of both?

"Jacob, there are only three flavors available at the ice cream store—pistachio, butter pecan, and chocolate peanut butter cup. Which do you choose?"

I figured I'd show him I was a traditionalist. I answered, "Butter pecan."

Justin's face turned solemn.

"But you're allergic to nuts, Jacob."

I told him I thought it was a theoretical question.

"No. It's a personal question. This is a personal interview. Let's move on."

"But I made the assumption that—" I began.

"Please, Jacob. Let's move on."

And move on we did. The next question was for Lindsay.

"If you could visit just one place in the world for a week, where would that place be?"

Oh, please don't say New York, sweetie, I thought. I shouldn't have worried.

She answered: "The moon."

"Interesting...now, Megan, are you still in touch with any of your friends from elementary school?"

"Megan, tell me one thing about Jacob that no one else in the room knows."

"Alex, what was your favorite toy as a child?"

"Jacob, tell me two things about your wife that you find extremely irritating."

"Megan, what's your ideal weight?"

"Alex, do you care if someone is gay or lesbian?"

"Jacob, if you could only wear a shirt of the same color for the rest of your life, what would that color be?"

And so it went: sports teams, jobs, religion, sex, animals, food, education, the future, the past, and, finally, the Store.

"Is the Store perfect?"

Megan said, "Almost."

Alex said, "I really don't know."

Lindsay said, "I guess so."

"And you, Jacob. Is the Store perfect?"

"Nothing on earth is perfect."

CHAPTER 18

THE CAR ride home from the "testing center." The click of the doors locking. The click of the seat belts fastening. We were like a chorus bursting with the same inevitable question: "So what did you think?"

We all asked it almost at once, and everyone except Lindsay jumped to answer it. Lindsay said she was too fearful of cameras and recording devices in the car to have a conversation. But the rest of us? We couldn't wait to talk about the interview. The hell with surveillance.

Megan said, "It was both better and worse than I had imagined. And I don't think it should have been done as a group. What kind of kid wants to answer tough questions about his parents when the parents are right in the room?"

"I thought it was all creepy," Alex said. "Justin was creepy. The room was creepy. And the questions were stupid. What difference does it make if you want to play the trumpet or play baseball or whether you wish you were taller? I mean, the whole thing was just to make sure you want to be part of this stupid place."

I agreed with all their observations. And I said so. It was creepy and embarrassing...and also exhausting. Hours of questions about your past, present, and future. Then I added a useless comment: "Well, at least it's over." But of course I knew I was lying, and they knew I was lying.

That's when Lindsay spoke. "Is it really over, Daddy? Won't there just be more bullshit? More nonsense? We take down the cameras, and they put them back up. They know you have a nut allergy. They know what toothpaste we use. They..." But then she squeezed her eyes tight. The tears seeped out anyway.

"Come on, sweetie," Megan said, unbuckling her seat belt and reaching toward the backseat. She took Lindsay's hand and squeezed it.

"Look. Once your mother and I..." I started to say, but was interrupted by Alex, whose voice was loud and high.

"Speaking of books: holy shit! Will you look at that?"

I pulled over and slammed on the brakes. To our left was the town library, which Megan and I had visited a few days earlier. Only something was very different: the library had been closed down.

Wooden boards covered the windows. A thick steel chain and a few big padlocks prevented anyone from entering. The flagpoles held no flags. Even the lawn was suddenly scraggly and in need of watering.

"What's going on?" Megan asked.

"I don't know," I answered. "But whatever it is...it's sure as hell not good."

We all looked at it for a few seconds, then I twisted myself around to face all three members of my family.

"Get out of the car. Everybody. Now. This minute," I said.

They looked frightened, but they moved fast. Within seconds we were on the cracked sidewalk in front of the derelict little building.

"You think there's a bomb in the car, Dad?" Alex asked.

"No," I said. "But I'm sure there's some sort of hidden recording device."

Their faces were filled with anxiety.

"Listen, and listen carefully. This town isn't a game or a joke. This place is scary as hell. From now on—and I really don't know what else to say—from now on we've all got to be very, very careful."

I watched as Alex fought to hold back his tears.

I watched as Megan drew the children close to her.

"I'm sorry, Daddy," said Lindsay. "But I'm really scared."

"That makes three of us, sweetie," Megan said.

"No," I said. "That makes four of us."

CHAPTER 19

WE HAVE friends whose apartments have been burglarized. They all say the same thing: "It feels like we've been violated."

I was learning how those friends must have felt. It seemed like every time we left our house, somebody or some*thing* from the Store came in. When we arrived home in the late afternoon after our "interview," we discovered that it had happened once again.

We walked into our house, and Megan said, "Looks like we're having barbecue for dinner." Sure enough, on the kitchen counter were a platter of pork ribs, a bowl of mashed sweet potatoes, and squares of buttered cornbread.

The only thing that amazed me was this: we weren't amazed. We were beginning to realize that being violated was part of life in New Burg.

Our intruders must have had a busy time in our house. The broken hinges on the coat closet had been tightened; the clean clothes in the laundry room had been folded and put away. Megan said, "This is sort of sick. Someone—a person I don't even know—is touching... well, touching my underpants, and it's just perverted."

"Violated," I said. "It makes you feel violated." Megan shook her head.

Then Alex spoke. As was often the case, he was standing in front of the open refrigerator.

"Hey, Mom, remember how I asked you to drone in some Mountain Dew the next time you were droning in groceries, and you said no?"

"What I actually said was...no way. It has too much sugar in it."

"I read that it has one cup of corn syrup in every twelve ounces," Professor Lindsay added.

"Well, whoever's been sneaking around here doesn't seem to agree. There's two six-packs of Dew in the fridge."

Upstairs the beds had been made. Our bathroom cabinet had been stocked with Megan's special prescription soap. The...then I stopped taking inventory and said, "Oh, shit. I gotta go see something."

I ran up the attic stairs. To our "book office." And sure enough, our messy piles of index cards had been straightened out. A new box of toner sat on the floor next to the printer. And—holy shit!—they had put an air conditioner in the tiny window near our work desk.

"Megan," I shouted. "Come up here!"

"I can't. Someone's at the back door."

By the time I'd made it down both flights of stairs, Megan and Lindsay were walking quickly toward the kitchen.

"Did you see on the monitor who's at the door?" I said.

"Who do you think? It's Fred and Ethel."

"Who are Fred and Ethel?" Lindsay said.

"Forget it, honey. It was before your time," Megan said.

"Hell. It was before *our* time."

Megan opened the door for Bette and Bud. Hugs and kisses all around.

"Heard you were having barbecue tonight. Thought we'd invite ourselves over. But we come bearing gifts, too," Bud said.

"Homemade peach pie and a bowl of *real* whipped cream," Bette said.

We didn't bother asking how they knew what our dinner plans were. We had already learned by then that the magical Store tablets disseminated whatever information they wanted people to know.

We settled down in the living room, and all four of us had a glass of Jackie D, as Bud called the Jack Daniel's bourbon he seemed to love so much.

"Nothing like an icy Jackie D and ginger ale on a hot night."

Damn it, I thought. *I have a question, and I'm going to ask it.* Yeah, I knew the surveillance cameras were whirling away. I knew there was no such thing as privacy in our own home. I didn't really care. So I asked.

"When you guys are away from your house, like shopping or at work…well, do people come in and do stuff? Change stuff? Like make the bed or put new grouting in the bathtub?"

Both Bette and Bud chuckled. But I could swear that there was a kind of nervousness behind their laughter.

"When we first got here stuff like that happened all the time. But then it stopped, and I think it's 'cause they figured out we're too ornery to care," Bud said.

"We're not the cooperative types by nature," Bette added.

A strange pause stopped the conversation. Then Bette broke the silence.

"Of course, this is New Burg. So you can't be sure when we say something that we're telling the truth," she said.

Another awkward pause. Megan took a sip of her Jackie D. Then she spoke.

"And of course you can't assume that Jacob and I are telling the truth, either."

"Well, I guess not," Bud said.

Then all four of us laughed.

Megan didn't have to say anything else. I knew what she was thinking.

Ugga-bugga.

CHAPTER 20

BETTE AND Bud went home right after dinner, but we were happy to see that half a peach pie remained. Alex and Lindsay wandered into their worlds of Facebook and Instagram. And Megan and I went to work in our newly air-conditioned attic office. It was almost eleven o'clock, but we had the energy of two people who were just beginning their day.

"This is the thing I've been wanting to show you all night," Megan said as she tapped furiously away at her laptop.

"Don't look over my shoulder," she said. "I want to have it all up on the screen."

After a few more seconds of my pretending not to look over her shoulder, she said, "Okay, now you can look. But understand. This isn't one big document. I simply cut and pasted a bunch of stuff I had downloaded and put all the pieces in one file. I'm calling the file LOLB."

"I give up. What does LOLB stand for?"

"Lots of legal bullshit."

"Oh, I should have been able to guess that," I said sarcastically, but she was ignoring me.

"Go ahead, now," she said. "Take a look."

It was extraordinary.

Bottom line: twenty-seven states had passed legislation that was clearly designed to be favorable to the Store. Oh, sure, the words *the Store* were never mentioned, but Megan and I knew what was going on.

The Connecticut General Assembly had passed what was listed as a "consumer beneficiary act." It prohibited any "land-based establishment" (that meant any brick-and-mortar store) from "reissuing pricing to coordinate with online offers without a seven-day interval."

Translation: if the Store had a Black & Decker power drill on sale for twenty-nine dollars, the town hardware store had to wait seven days before it could lower its price to match the Store's.

In Chicago, the aldermen had passed an act that was "designed for the financial improvement of the low-income housing access incentive," allowing the city to give "free-of-charge electronic tablets and computers to all households with incomes below twenty-four thousand dollars. Within the first three months, said tablets and computers will only be able to access websites with retail marketing content."

Translation: the poor people of Chicago could get crappy free computers programmed only to allow them to visit sites where they could buy stuff. That would mean supermarkets and other big box stores, but it would overwhelmingly mean that they'd be clicking on the Store site, buying all sorts of shit they couldn't afford and getting deeper into credit card debt.

The pro-Store amendments and acts and laws rolled on and on.

Not surprisingly, Nebraska had more pro-Store acts than any other state. It was as if Nebraska were preparing for a day when the Store would rule the state. The legislature in Lincoln had enacted environmentally dangerous rules in preparation for a time when the skies would be so blackened by drones that millions of trees would have to be cut down.

In Florida it was assumed that Cubans would soon be flocking in huge numbers to South Florida, so why not pass a law that allowed "temporary" immigrants to be paid less than minimum wage? That's what the state senate in Tallahassee did.

The new air conditioner was working hard, but it could not stop our blood from boiling.

"This makes me want to vomit," I said.

"And that's putting it nicely," Megan said.

Megan said that she would forward me the entire file immediately. Then she very wisely suggested that we hand-copy the information onto index cards and erase all electronic evidence from our computers. We both assumed that electronic spying was more likely than conducting a home invasion in order to steal hard copy. (Yeah, I know. Never assume.)

"When I say 'erase,' I mean *erase*," Megan said.

Not a problem for us. One of Megan's "freelance from hell" jobs was writing a ten-page instruction booklet called "Ten Computer Hacks That Anyone Can Learn." So she knew how to scrub a computer *completely* clean, way beyond the useless "Clear History" procedure that most of us amateurs use. (Yeah, I know this, too. There's no such thing as completely clean.)

Before I dug into the LOLB file, I pursued a Store-related project of my own. I had taken on the job of assembling information on the original founder of the Store. You'd think it would be easy to google and surf your way to a pile of facts about Thomas P. Owens, but information was shockingly scarce. Owens was born in Lorain, Ohio, in 1939. That made him around seventy-eight years old now. He was living in Arizona, and he owned another residence in New York City. He had founded the Store about twenty years ago. It was a sloppy-looking, primitive website where Owens sold books, office supplies, and, of all things, long-forgotten candy brands like Necco Wafers and Bonomo Turkish Taffy.

The business (then called Your Store) was successful enough to rate an article in the *Wall Street Journal* and *Crain's New York Business*. In 1998 Owens sold the Store to an investment group.

And I couldn't find a damn thing about the guy from that day on.

My fingers were dancing on the keyboard when Megan said, "Have you read the file on the LOLB stuff?"

"Not yet. I'm about to. I was just doing some follow-ups on Thomas P. Owens."

"Yeah. Well, drop everything, buddy, and step over here. This is going to knock your head off."

CHAPTER 21

CONFIDENTIAL
READ THE FOLLOWING
BEFORE PROCEEDING

This electronic communication is for your eyes only. It will self-destruct within an hour of its opening. It is immune from forwarding, printing, and alteration. It is photography-immune. While some readers may wish to copy part or all of this communication, any publicized content will be categorically denied by the sender.

RECIPIENTS: Senator Kathleen Langston, Senator Julio Ramiro Munoz, Senator Franklin Peterson, Senator Dominick Roselli

FROM: Senator William Ward

SUBJECT: Constitutional Amendment XXVIII

This will serve as the final follow-up to our conversation of last Tuesday at the Four Seasons Hotel.

At that meeting it was decided to advance the cause of a constitutional amendment abolishing all sales tax on consumer goods purchased over the Internet if more than 50 percent of the goods in any given purchase are manufactured in the United States.

I am pleased to report that I have had several conversations with Roger Kendrick, CEO and president of TheStore.com. He has endorsed the idea enthusiastically.

Gathering votes for a constitutional amendment is no small task, yet polls that TheStore.com has conducted privately indicate that it can be accomplished. As such, I am suggesting we create a call-on list of our Senate colleagues and, further, that we designate two of us to visit the Oval Office.

I have made arrangements for our specific group of five to meet secretly Sunday evening at 8:00 p.m. in suite PH3 at the Ritz-Carlton in Georgetown.

Accomplishing our goal of passage of Amendment XXVIII will be great for America, great for TheStore.com, and great for the five of us.

WW/pb

As I read the secret memorandum on the computer screen, my arms and legs were actually shaking. The only thing I could say was the ever-useful "Holy shit!" And I said it more than once.

"Is this for real?" I asked.

"For real."

"Double holy shit!"

Members of the US Senate were plotting to add an amendment to the Constitution that would make the Store the most important and profitable company in America—and probably the world.

I grasped Megan's shoulders gently. "How'd you get this?" I asked.

Without missing a beat, she said, "I hacked it."

"You hacked it?" I said. "When did—"

"Don't, Jacob. Don't ask. Don't worry about it. I just learned," she said.

This skill seemed way more advanced than the information in her computer hacking booklet.

"Megan, this is serious shit. We could get killed for this," I said.

She stood up and faced me.

"No, Jacob. This is serious shit because five senators are totally screwing with the people of the United States. This is serious shit because the Store is on some weird goddamn track to...I don't know...take over the world. Are we going to do this research right or not? If the answer is no, then let's get the hell back to New York and forget about New Burg and the Store and our book."

I moved in closer to Megan. I hugged her, and I put my face down into her neck and kissed her.

"You're right, of course," I said. "And you're married to a wuss, and you don't deserve what I—"

"Oh, stop it. We're going to do this. We're going to look into this until we either break the Store wide open *or* they..."

She hesitated, just for a moment.

"Or they what?" I said.

"Or they kill us."

CHAPTER 22

OUR JOBS at the fulfillment center were backbreakingly painful *and* mind-numbingly dull—load the Stormer with merchandise, and when the vehicle could hold no more stuff, unload it at the packing center. Then do it again and again and again and...

Quite quickly, however, Megan's job became much easier than mine. You see, Sam Reed, the group manager who handed out the loading assignments, had taken a very smarmy liking to Megan. So while I was usually assigned to lifting and packing cow manure, industrial-size sacks of cake flour, even barbells, Megan was mostly assigned to books, cosmetics, and greeting cards.

Sam called Megan "my sweet Irish colleen" and "my copper-haired beauty." He usually rested his skinny hairy hands on her shoulders when he spoke to her, and once he even suggested that it was unnecessary for her to keep the top button on her Store uniform closed. This suggestion was followed by a creepy "Guys love playing peek-a-breast." Yeah, Sam was a class act.

If this were another company, Megan would have been lodging a complaint with human resources, but we kept reminding each other that the long-term purpose of our jobs was to gather not just Bose headphones and Huggies and folding chairs but also information that would tell America the truth about the Store.

Megan and I were driving home from work the day after we had barbecue with Bette and Bud.

"Am I losing all sense of time in this crazy place?" Megan asked. "Or did we not just have dinner with Bette and Bud?"

She was reading the evening schedule on her tablet.

"Yeah," I said. "Barbecue plus half a bottle of Jackie D."

"Well, guess what? There's a message here. They have a seven o'clock reservation at the Minka Japanese Restaurant in town, and they're expecting us to meet them there for dinner," Megan said.

"How'd they know we were free?" I asked.

"How? You know how. Everyone's schedule is published, and I guess we failed to put something down for seven o'clock. So they rightly assume we're free."

An hour later we were sitting at the Minka with Bette and Bud as well as a huge platter of sushi, a plateful of chicken teriyaki, and some deep-fried pork cutlets. A person might lose his mind living in New Burg, but he'd never lose weight.

"Is Minka the name of the people who own the store, do you think?" I asked.

"No," said Bette. "Minka is a basic farmhouse-type building style that the Japanese use. When I designed the

restaurant I thought the rustic look would be very soothing."

"When *you* designed it?" Megan said. She did not do
a very good job of hiding her surprise that this simple-
sounding woman in her simple yellow sundress was ... an
architect?

"Yep. I know I don't seem the type. But I am an architect."

It turned out that Bette had planned and designed almost half the stores and restaurants in New Burg. She had
a degree from Carnegie Mellon. She had done an intern-
ship at Skidmore, Owings & Merrill.

"And I suppose you're chairman of neurosurgery,
Bud?" I said with a laugh.

"Afraid not. Bette's the brains of this duo. I'm a security
guard at the chemical warehouse at the fulfillment center,"
he said.

"We drive past that warehouse on our way to work
every day," I said.

Bud said, "Because of my security pass, me and Bette
were able to get in and see you both on your first day at
the job."

"Now, listen," Bette said very gently. "I have a favor to
ask of you two."

"Sure," Megan said. "Anything."

"Oh, this'll be easy," Bette said. "Just don't go telling
other people you know that I'm the architect—"

"Or that I'm a security guard."

"But other people must already know," Megan said.

"Some do. Some don't," said Bette. "We believe the less

said the better. That should be the eleventh commandment in New Burg."

Shit! They were nervous. They were about as paranoid as anyone could be, even in New Burg. So whether they were friends or not, whether they were spies or not...I had to ask.

"What are you two so afraid of?"

There was a pause.

"Everything. Absolutely everything," Bud said.

After that answer, there really wasn't anything more to say.

Near the window a drone hovered in the air. Had the window been open, the drone could have snatched a piece of sushi.

Bette and Bud looked at each other. They smiled at each other. Then they waved hello to the drone.

CHAPTER 23

IT WAS the first week of school. And we were dreading it.

We knew how Lindsay and Alex felt about leaving their teachers and their friends back in New York—that we'd been selfish in uprooting them. We knew because they never let us forget it.

We also knew that as two savvy, jaded New York kids, they were bound to be negative and sarcastic about a high school in Nebraska. So we were prepared for the worst when they came home from their first day at New Burg High.

"How was school?" Megan asked—steeling herself for the complaints, the accusations, the guilt.

"Kind of cool," said Alex.

"Way cool," Lindsay added. "Do you know that they give every kid a brand-new cell phone? Look!" She took one out of her backpack. "And we can load it up with all the apps we want—free. Anything that isn't X-rated."

"Plus look—we each got our own new laptop," Alex added. "So you can junk the one I brought with me."

That laptop, state of the art a year ago, didn't hold a candle to the new one Alex had in his hands, outfitted with all the best bells and whistles Silicon Valley could create. Alex showed me that the laptop had a flexible screen that could be creased and rolled into a cylinder. When he showed me that it had "retinal access," so you didn't need a password, I thought I had landed in the year 2040 ... or maybe the year 2040 had already landed in New Burg.

Okay. So it stood to reason that any school connected to the Store would be a mecca of high-end electronics. So much for the first day, as both kids disappeared into their rooms to explore their new gadgets.

But day 2 surprised us even more.

They still loved it.

I mean ... they *really* loved it.

They loved it like nothing they'd ever loved before. Even the ridiculously expensive private schools they had attended back in New York.

They loved the teachers. They loved the students. They loved the classes. They loved the school sports teams, the school colors, even the food in the cafeteria. ("Dad, they've even got an authentic sushi chef.")

As the days went on, we kept hearing about "this cool computer science teacher" and "this cool soccer coach" and "this cool girl with this really cool ladybug tattoo on the back of her neck."

Megan and I were silent for the first week or so. But something was clearly wrong.

"Okay. Here goes," Megan nervously said to me one

night. "I never thought I'd say this in a million years. But I think the kids are liking school way, way too much."

Ordinarily we would have laughed at such a wacky observation. But she was right. And it scared us.

"Could they be lying to make us feel good?" I asked.

"They rarely lie. And they rarely care how we feel," she said.

"The other thing is that they seem to have so many more friends than they did back in New York."

And that was true. Alex and Lindsay were bringing home new friends every day. Kids with big wide smiles on big, good-looking faces. I had taken to calling them the Smileys. Smiley Jason, Smiley Andrew, Smiley Emma...

"I know I'm going to sound like a crazy lady," Megan said. "But teenagers *shouldn't be so happy.*"

Our kids were changed, all right. But it was starting to feel like a change for the worse.

Our conversation came to a quick halt when Alex walked into the room.

"Hey," he said. "When's dinner? I've got to be at my friend Nathan's in half an hour. By the way, did Lindsay tell you about the Life Program e-mails we both got?"

"Life Program?" Megan said as she put the vegetables in the microwave. "Sounds like a plan for healthy eating."

"No. It's awesome—really," said Alex. "We took a bunch of tests on the second day of school, and they have some people who figure out from the tests, like, what a kid would be good at. And they arrange your whole school experience—that's what they call it. Like, for me, they said I tested really well to be a doctor. So they want me to join Chem Club and get training for the New Burg Emergency Rescue Unit and take a bunch of special bio courses. And—if you can believe it—they said that Lindsay would be, like, a marketing genius when she grows up. So she should take all these extra courses they give in—I don't know, like, why people buy stuff and want stuff and dimbographics—"

"Demographics," Megan said.

"It sounds way too early in life to start planning that sort of stuff," I said. There was no anger in my voice, but there was certainly some anxiety in my heart.

"It sounds great to me," Alex said. "I mean, Dad, come on. You can't ever get started early enough. And these people at school know what they're doing."

Who was this kid talking? What happened to Alex?

"But Alex," Megan said. "You're just beginning to live your life. You can't know what you want to be or do or..."

"Yeah? Why not, Mom? Even Lindsay agrees. It makes a lot of sense."

He was smiling. He was wearing the same smile I saw on his friends. It was the charming but vacant smile, the "all's right with the world" smile. The New Burg smile.

"Call me when the food's on the table," he yelled as he left.

Alex was gone. Megan and I looked at each other. We didn't say anything for a few seconds.

Then I said, "Okay. Okay. I know it sounds a little crazy. But maybe we're overreacting. This could be a very good thing. It makes some sense."

"I kinda disagree. Jacob, the thing is called Life Program. Lindsay and Alex are kids. They're barely adolescents. And they're being *programmed. For life!*"

"Let's stay calm. Like I said, it could be a good thing."

"Do you really think so?" Megan asked.

I shook my head. Confused. Concerned.

"No, I don't."

Megan spoke again.

"Are they trying to take our kids away from us?"

I shook my head again.

"That's crazy, right? I mean...they couldn't really do that. Could they?"

Could they?

The microwave beeped. Megan called to Alex and Lindsay. They came running in quickly.

Both of them were smiling.

CHAPTER 24

THERE WAS a good reason why Megan and I had been selected to "help out" at the Special Arts Gathering. But we didn't know it at the time.

The shindig was to be held in the Executive Reception Hall. The guests: big-deal artists, designers, writers, and philosophers as well as some of the seldom-seen movers and shakers from the world of the Store.

The Executive Reception Hall was a dead ringer for Versailles: Fragonard-style murals, ornate (and probably authentic) Louis XIV furniture, gold-and-crystal chandeliers. At one end of the huge room was a stage with a lectern.

Mingling among the celebrities were around a hundred people who worked at the Store. I recognized nobody, but they were easy to spot. They all wore electronic ID badges that read: I'M WITH THE STORE. WELCOME.

After the guests had their fill of Champagne and hors d'oeuvres, the chandeliers flickered and the guests took their seats. Megan and I and the other six "helpers" scurried around like rats, collecting dirty plates, glasses, and napkins. Then we stood behind the seated assembly and watched.

A very attractive young woman wearing a very attractive navy-blue suit approached the lectern.

"Isabel Toledo," Megan whispered to me.

"That's her name?" I whispered back.

Megan rolled her eyes.

"No, idiot. That's who designed her suit."

"Oh."

"The Store Talks to the Arts lectures have been a huge success so far," she said. "Today, for the fifth in the series, we're delighted to have with us Dr. David Werner, the world-renowned economist and Kinkaid professor of economics at Harvard University."

The woman recited a few more of Dr. Werner's credentials and ended with this: "Dr. Werner's talk is entitled 'The Hidden and Surprising Influence of Art and Music on the Economic Recovery.'"

Then Dr. Werner took the stage: a frail-looking man of around seventy-five in a dark gray suit and bright blue bow tie.

We would quickly discover that there was nothing frail about him.

At first he said nothing. He took his time surveying the audience, his face stern, his head moving slowly from left to right. Then he spoke.

"I have been called upon to speak about art and music. And I am sure we would all enjoy a discussion on such noble pleasures. But that's not what I'm going to talk about. And if you don't like what I have to say, well, that's just too damn bad."

A few in the crowd looked at one another, some with concern, some with confusion. The woman who had introduced Dr. Werner abruptly stood from her front-row seat and left the auditorium. Dr. Werner continued.

"Let me make my point very clear at the outset." There was a pause. Then his voice boomed out over the crowd.

"I don't like you! At all! Any of you!"

There were a few scattered laughs in the audience. But Werner quickly silenced them with a swat of his hand.

"No—don't laugh," he continued. "In fact . . ." Another pause, and then even louder than before, "You all sicken me. This place sickens me. The Store makes me puke."

People in the audience looked at one another. Eyebrows shot up. Mouths shot open. A murmur. A few whispers.

I heard someone say, "It must be a joke."

But something inside me knew this was not a joke. This fire-and-brimstone preacher was there to preach.

The question was, would anyone other than Megan and I agree with him?

"Just look at the evil that you and the Store have unleashed," he shouted. "Not content to manipulate the general public by underselling and eliminating all competition in a free capitalist system, you and the Store have also become the world's primary gatherer of personal and private customer information."

The murmurs were growing louder. An occasional hiss shot out of the audience. I heard some hearty angry boos.

"The Store has captured the minds and wallets of America because it follows and records everything Americans do. They know what people search for, long for. They know and analyze everything people do online— whether tawdry or respectable. They know what Americans eat and when they eat it. They know what people watch and when they watch it. They even know when people screw and whom they screw..."

Megan and I looked at each other in amazement. This Werner guy was hurling bombs of truth at the audience—things we truly believed.

But the audience was having none of it. Two hulking thugs in cheap black suits appeared at either side of the stage.

But Dr. Werner wouldn't let up. With every sentence, he left Megan and me with faster heartbeats and happier hearts.

"The Store has lobbyists in Washington, DC, that number in the thousands," he said. "And a network of spies and counterspies who have infiltrated every state in the union, perhaps every country in the world," he added.

"I can only assume that the most basic protective agencies of government—organizations such as the FBI and the CIA—are complicit."

Megan and I looked around. Many in the audience were standing, shouting at Werner, "Get the hell out of here." Those who stayed seated were stamping their feet.

"And worst of all," he began—but he never got to finish.

The two black-suited thugs rushed toward him and

lifted him up by his armpits, hauling him offstage. As he tried to wriggle out of their grasp, the audience cheered.

"Don't say anything, Jacob," Megan said. "Don't look at him. Don't look at me. Don't smile. Let's just clear these dishes as if nothing had happened."

Of course she was right. Even the slightest reaction on our part could betray us as the rebels we knew we were.

"But I've got to meet this guy."

I worked my way to the front of the huge room, to the door that led to an offstage area. The pretty woman in the blue suit was in serious conversation with the two beefy-looking guys who had carried Werner off.

"Excuse me," I said. "I was wondering if you could direct me to Dr. Werner."

The three of them looked at one another for a moment.

"He's gone," the first man said.

"I know. I saw him ... uh ... leave the stage. I was hoping I could—"

"Gone," said the second man.

"Well, do you happen to know which way he went? Maybe there's a chance I could—"

"No," the woman said, cutting me off. She made a gesture with her hand.

"Dr. Werner ... is not with us anymore."

CHAPTER 25

IT'S 1984 ALL OVER AGAIN!

BARBECUE AT BETTE AND BUD'S

SUNDAY, 5:00 P.M.

That was Bette and Bud's e-vite.

Megan's reaction was the same as mine.

"Did it ever *stop* being 1984 in New Burg?" she asked.

Whatever the year, we showed up with a chocolate-marshmallow pie in our hands and a bunch of index cards in our back pockets.

"I think you already know at least half the folks here," Bette said.

She was right. Many of the twenty-odd people at the barbecue had helped us on moving day. One of them was suddenly standing right next to me.

I'm embarrassed to say that I remembered Mark Stanton because Mark and his wife, Cookie, were the only African Americans in that collection of white New Burg faces.

"My man Jacob," said Mark Stanton.

We bumped fists, and I said, "Where's Cookie?"

Mark shrugged, a vague nonanswer.

Meanwhile Megan was talking to Marie DiManno, the widow who seemed to have been the chief organizer of the help on our moving day.

A pretty woman distributed rum-laced drinks in plastic cups. Two handsome guys I didn't know played a lazy man's game of badminton.

For a moment I considered this: there were worse things than standing and sipping a cool drink on a warm Nebraska Sunday afternoon.

But that happy moment passed quickly. I also knew that there was a video camera beneath the picnic table and at least three other cameras attached to the gutters of the house. I recognized one of the men tending the charcoal grill as one of the two guys who had hustled Dr. Werner offstage. I watched audio-video drones swooping in and around small groupings of party guests. And I couldn't help but wonder why Mark Stanton had not given me a simple straight answer when I'd asked about his wife.

It took us about an hour to devour all the steak (excellent) and ribs (extraordinary) that Bette and Bud had served up. By 7:00 p.m. we had polished off the last remnants of chocolate-marshmallow pie and coconut cream cake. Two blackberry pies had also disappeared. The video cameras were recording lots of people groaning in satisfaction.

Who knew that the evening was just beginning?

One of the guests, a nice-looking mom type who

worked at the fulfillment center, tapped a spoon against a coffee cup and spoke.

"You all know me. I'm Lynn Harris. And you all know what time it is, right?" she said.

Everyone except Megan and I seemed to know. Everyone else began applauding and letting out whoops and cheers.

"That's right. It's the perfect moment for Store Talk," she said. Then she looked directly at Megan and me.

"I think our new neighbors need to be told about Store Talk. Don't be scared, you two. We pick a bunch of topics that are sort of meaningful to New Burg and the Store. Then we put the topics in a little bag, pull one topic out, and have a discussion. We keep doing that until we all get tired or somebody gets nasty."

Lynn laughed. Then she added, "I wrote out the topics this time."

I couldn't keep my mouth shut, of course. "You thought up the topics and put them in the bag or you were *given* the topics and put them in the bag?"

One of the guys who had been playing badminton said, "Little bit of each. It doesn't really make any difference where the topics come from."

"It sounds like a lot of fun," Megan said.

I was both proud and nervous to be married to a wife who could lie so convincingly.

"Megan, you draw the first topic," Lynn said. Then she added, "And Jacob, you can read it to us."

The crowd applauded, and Bud yelled, "Go on, Megan. Pick a good one."

In a few seconds, Megan handed me a piece of paper.

Then I read the first Store Talk subject to the crowd.

"Pawnee Preservation," I read. Then I added, "Maybe it's supposed to say 'reservation,' not 'preservation.'"

"No. It's right," said a chubby middle-aged guy. "There's a big to-do about this Indian burial ground they found when they started digging for the new water fluoridation and vitamin-enhancement plant. Some folks think it should be left alone, and some folks think, oh, what the hell. The Indians—"

"Native Americans," Mark Stanton said, correcting him.

"Yeah, Native Americans . . . are all gone."

"Well, I don't think it's rightly our decision," said Marie DiManno. "The Store people should decide stuff like that."

Now Bette spoke. She was cheerful, but her voice was firm: "Right. Why should we have a part in any decision?" Sure, Megan and I realized Bette was being sarcastic, but I wondered how many others did.

I watched as Bud gently tapped his wife's hand, a kind of "Calm down, honey" gesture.

"Give us another topic, Megan. Try to make it a bit less controversial," Bud said.

"I'll try my best," said Megan. Soon I had another phrase to read.

"Cornhusker football!"

Where I come from, a sports "discussion" could lead to screams, threats, and pistols at dawn. I soon found out it wasn't much different in New Burg.

"They're a bunch of freakin' losers this year," said one slightly paunchy guy who, ironically, was wearing a Nebraska T-shirt.

"They're looking like winners to me," said the security guard from the Werner lecture.

Then Bud spoke up. His voice was a little too loud for comfort.

"Yeah, they're winners. As long as they don't play Ohio State, Michigan State, Penn State, or Wisconsin." Laughter from most of the group.

But one young guy disagreed enough to stand up and say angrily, "Who the hell are you? Joe Buck?"

Another young guy shot up and said, "Watch your language, Carl. There are women here."

"Let's all stay calm and friendly," Lynn said. "It's only football."

A new voice yelled, *Only? Only football?*

I watched as one couple headed toward the driveway.

Lynn spoke. She was clearly nervous. "I'm going to have Megan keep picking until we get something that we can have a civil discussion about."

The group had quieted down, but almost no one was smiling.

Lynn put the bag in front of Megan once again.

Megan pulled out a slip of paper and handed it to me.

I read aloud, "Dr. David Werner."

A few "Who?" and "Who's that?" murmurs came from the crowd.

I answered. "He's the guy who spoke at the arts gathering the other day. He's the guy who was dissing the Store."

"I heard about him. He's a lunatic," one woman said.

"My wife was helping out at the place. She said that the guy was a maniac. They even had to pull him off the stage."

The crowd was stirring now. Mumblings of people exchanging ideas. Some of them pretty loud.

"He sounds like a real asshole."

"Yeah. If you live here, then you know what the deal is. You go with the Store. It's their town."

"Well, I can't say I agree with this Werner's point of view, but he does have the right to—" said one foolishly courageous woman.

Some other woman shot back immediately: "He sure as hell doesn't have the right to come in here and shoot off his mouth. He's probably one of these egghead types who's jealous of our lives here."

Then Bette stood up. Her voice was calm but strong.

She said, "I think Werner made a lot of good points."

A sudden silence came over everyone. Bette surveyed the crowd quickly, her face a mix of confusion and anger.

"What's wrong with all of you? Are you so afraid of the Store that you can't even express an opinion at a backyard barbecue?"

"We're not *afraid*. We're happy," yelled Mark Stanton. "Is that so awful?"

Bette responded immediately. "Lemme ask you this. Is your wife, Cookie, happy, too? Is she so happy that we never see her anymore?"

"Bud, get your wife to shut up," an older man shouted.

Lynn Harris then joined the noise. "There's no place in

all of America that's as good as this. Forgive me if I just take my shopping bag and leave."

Lynn Harris and her husband and another two couples walked toward the driveway.

"Don't you get it, Bette? We like living here. We think it's pretty damn perfect," said one of the badminton guys.

And then it happened.

Bette looked directly at Megan and me and said, "You guys know what I'm talking about. Right? We've got to get some limitations put on the Store. Our lives are *our* lives. You agree with me? Right?"

We didn't answer.

Bud joined her. "Come on. You know she's right. You know that. Don't you? Jacob, Megan. Say something."

But we didn't.

We had a horrible choice. Megan and I could say what we thought and blow our cover, or we could simply lie and move ahead with our book.

Then Mark Stanton lost his very smooth coolness and shouted. "This is all bullshit, Bette. We'd have nothing if we didn't have the Store."

People were agreeing loudly, and more people began leaving. Some left quietly with a few polite farewells. Others left curtly, without so much as a good-bye.

"What should we do?" Megan said quietly to me.

"We should try to remember everything that's happening here right now. Then go home and write it all down."

CHAPTER 26

CARS WERE leaving the driveway quickly, as if they were fleeing a disaster. Only Marie remained. She was talking to Bette and Bud.

We heard Marie say, "Thanks for the party. But you guys'll have to learn when to keep your mouths closed. I'll come get my bowls tomorrow."

And then there were four. Bette and Bud. Megan and I.

"Well, thanks," I said. "It was really interesting. Fun and interesting."

Bette looked at Megan sadly.

"Did you really think so? The problem is—" but she was interrupted by a man's voice coming from the other end of the backyard.

"Excuse me, folks," the man said. Now we saw two police officers—one male, one female. They were walking toward us.

"We got some complaints about noise coming from a party here," the man said.

Bud—gruff and unhappy—spoke up. "It's only a bar-becue. How noisy could it be?"

"Are you the owner of this residence?" the male officer said.

"Yeah, we both are," said Bette.

"Well, it might be time to send the guests home and start the cleanup," the officer said.

"We're the only guests left," I said.

"And we were just leaving," Megan added.

Both of us gave dumb little smiles to Bette and Bud. The police began heading back toward one end of the yard.

"Wait. Wait. Wait," Bud shouted. "Megan, Jacob. I just want to say one thing to you guys."

There was a pause. Bette was looking at the ground. Bud's eyes were wet.

"Promise me," Bud said. "Promise me you won't be-come like the rest of them."

Before I could say anything, Bette spoke.

"Bud, honey, don't ask them to make promises they can't keep."

CHAPTER 27

MEGAN AND I had plenty of juicy material to tran-scribe when we got home that night. We stayed up until well past 2:00 a.m., which may not have been the smartest idea. The next day was Monday, our early day. On Mondays we had to check in at the fulfillment cen-ter at 7:00 a.m.

"We've got a few minutes," I said to Megan as we turned in to our designated entry gate. "I'm going to see if we can stop by and see Bud at the chemical warehouse."

"They'll never let you visit a site that's not approved for you," Megan said.

She was probably right, but I wanted to give it a try. Plus I have enormous faith in my own powers of bullshit. So we gave the hundreds of surveillance cameras quite the workout. With the help of the Store Driving Assist app we pulled up in front of a security gate at the chemical ware-house around fifteen minutes later.

My electronically embedded entrance pass did not budge the steel gate. But it did, apparently, notify three security guards that people who had not been properly cleared were trying to get in.

"You folks lost?" said the small nervous-looking woman, accompanied by two male guards, who came out front to meet us.

"No. We know we're at the chemical warehouse. I wanted to drop by for a second before work and deliver a message to our friend Bud."

Megan spoke up. "We work at the fulfillment center."

"What's Bud's last name?" the woman asked.

"Robinson. Bud may not be his real first name. It could be a nickname."

The woman was pressing keys on her tablet.

"Nobody named Robinson here. Bud or otherwise," she said.

The two men were also pressing keys on their tablets. One of them said, "Wait a sec. Was this guy a security guard?"

"Where'd you see that?" the woman asked.

"He's on the T list," he said.

"Yes, he's a security guard," I said.

"Yeah, the T list," the woman said. "He and his wife are being transferred."

"What the hell does that mean?" I said way too loudly. I was feeling the same angry confusion I had felt when the librarian told us that her husband had been transferred, with no explanation.

"It means that the husband and wife have been transferred. Sometimes they send transfer candidates to the main office, in San Francisco, for debriefing before reassignment," one of the men said. Then the woman spoke.

"If I were you two, I'd get over to your jobs at the fulfillment center. You don't want to be late, Megan. You don't either, Jacob. Put in a good day's work. Then get on home to make a nice dinner for Alex and Lindsay."

We were becoming so used to everyone knowing everything about us that we weren't surprised that she knew our names.

All Megan and I knew was this: less than twelve hours after their barbecue, Bette and Bud were being transferred or had been transferred or were being debriefed before they were transferred.

Megan and I decided that we would be late for work.

CHAPTER 28

WE PULLED into Bette and Bud's driveway like two high-way patrolmen on a chase. Even the brakes screeched as we made a fast stop and then walked quickly to the front door.

Doorbell. Short wait. A thirtyish woman, pretty enough, in jeans and a turquoise T-shirt, a headband holding her blond hair back. Since so many of the residents of New Burg looked like they could be related, I thought that possibly this woman was related to Bette. A cousin, maybe?

"Hey," I said. "Sorry to bother you so early in the day, but is Bud or Bette around?"

"Who?"

"Oh, we're the Brandeises. I'm Megan. He's my husband, Jacob."

"Hi," she said sweetly. "But what I meant is, who is it you're looking for?"

I was becoming as confused as the woman. "Bette and Bud Robinson. They live here."

"You must have the wrong house. I'm Tess Morris. My husband, Peter, and I just moved in here with our kids."

"When?" Megan asked. "When did you move in?"

"We flew in last night. We slept on some air mattresses, and the moving truck is out back, unloading our furniture. A few new neighbors even came by to help. I thought you might be part of that group."

There was a pause. All three of us were feeling awkward.

A man—quite tall, dark curly hair—walked in behind the woman at the door.

"Hi," he said. "I'm Pete Morris. We just moved in. What can I do for you?"

Tess Morris explained what our visit was about, that we were "mistakenly looking for a couple who don't live here."

"They were living here yesterday," Megan said. "We went to a barbecue . . . right here, early last night."

"I doubt it," said Pete. He was developing that "Are you crazy or what?" attitude. "There's not even a barbecue grill out back. I looked. And the rooms are all freshly painted. Come on in. You can get a whiff of the fresh paint."

We stepped inside. We'd been in this front hallway before. When Bette and Bud lived here it was painted a pale mint-green color. Now it was beige. I looked through the narrow passage that led to the kitchen. I saw Marie DiManno carrying a large cardboard moving carton. A moment later I watched Mark Stanton carrying a big crystal lamp.

"Yeah," I said. "The paint *does* smell fresh. The place

looks great. But I've got to ask just one more time. You two never heard of Bette and Bud Robinson?"

"No. Never heard of them," Pete said.

Megan to the rescue.

"Well, whatever. Welcome to the neighborhood. We'll be by with a pie or a casserole or something. Really. Welcome," she said.

"Thanks," Tess Morris said. "I think this town is going to be perfect for us."

Just before we turned toward the open door, I said, "Yes. I think this place will be absolutely perfect for you."

CHAPTER 29

WE STIFLED any ideas we might have had about looking into Bette and Bud's disappearance. We had heard at the fulfillment center that there were two debriefing centers, one in San Francisco and one in Atlanta. But we didn't know how to begin, let alone where to begin. And with our day jobs at the Store and our night jobs on our book project, we were already running on only four or five hours of sleep a night.

The day job was stupid. Megan and I never got tired of complaining to each other about it. The work was hard. It was uninteresting. It was boring. Driving our Stormers around the vast fulfillment center was also surprisingly exhausting.

But the job had important advantages. We could fade anonymously into the routine of the thousands of people who worked at the Store and move easily among our fellow workers. Megan's sweet personality made her especially adept at getting people to relax and open up, sometimes with some juicy inside information about the goings-on at the Store. But even that was scary. Were our informants telling us the truth? Were they reporting back to some higher-ups that we were digging around for information? Who the hell ever knew what the real deal was at the Store?

And after just weeks on the job, in spite of the aches in our backs and the dullness in our brains, we were on our way to a great book.

"Look," I would often say. "A year from now we'll be back in New York, sitting on top of the world."

Megan would agree. Then she would say that we were going to be found out, that she and I and Alex and Lindsay would disappear from the face of the earth. We'd talk. We'd even cry sometimes. And then we did the only thing we could: we'd get back to work on the book.

So when the notice went out on everyone's personal message boards that the job of assistant group manager, reporting to Sam Reed, was available, Megan and I never even considered applying.

A few days later, while loading twenty cartons of environmentally friendly lightbulbs and three hundred cases of Fancy Feast Classic cat food on my Stormer, I received the following text message from Megan:

Unbelievable! They promoted me to the Asst Mgr job!

When Megan and I spoke at lunch, I said that I was shocked; she hadn't even applied for the job.

Megan said, "I would have been shocked, too... *except*

our asshole manager Sam Reed is the one who told me about it. He said it was mainly his decision. He said it's because I have 'such a sweet attitude.'"

"And such a sweet ass," I added.

We both laughed. But let's face it. This kind of thing never makes a husband happy.

Megan and I agreed that the best way to proceed would be to act grateful to Sam and try to create more opportunities to get information for our book. So at the little congratulatory party for Megan (a few hundred people, exquisite Lafite Rothschild Bordeaux, and the same little caviar treats they'd served at Dr. Werner's rant), when Sam raised his glass to toast Megan and said, "Who'd have thought we'd welcome so much sunshine from New York?" Megan smiled.

Then she said, "I can't think of a nicer place to shine than right here in New Burg."

And the Oscar for best performance by a woman in a leading role goes to Megan Brandeis.

I couldn't help but think—at least for a second—that tomorrow Megan would be behind a desk and I'd be behind the wheel of a Stormer. Then I glanced toward the front of the room and watched Sam Reed and Megan. They were posing for photos. Phone cameras were clicking all over the place. I watched as Sam put his arm around the back of Megan's waist. I watched his hand inch slowly down to a place it shouldn't be. I watched and waited for Megan to push Sam's hand away. It didn't happen. Maybe she had to let Sam hold her. But then again, maybe she didn't.

My paranoia was not over the edge, but it sure as hell was heading in that direction.

I decided that all would be well for a while. Maybe I was being stupidly influenced by all those signs around the fulfillment centers that said NO WORRIES.

CHAPTER 30

"ALEX, YOU can turn off that damn camera *right now*," Megan said. Her voice meant business.

We had both spotted Alex and Lindsay in our workroom-office, hiding behind a stack of old issues of the *Wall Street Journal*. They were making yet another video of us on their flat-vids, the little slim steel contraptions that let them text, phone, record, and edit videos.

For the past three days they had been shooting us non-stop. They shot us having coffee in the morning. They shot us on the phone, at the supermarket, washing the car, everywhere but in the shower and on the john—and I wasn't even sure we had escaped that humiliation. They told us, "We even have lots of great shots of you guys sleeping."

They said it was for a school project called Home Sweet New Burg.

"It's a collage-type thing," Alex explained. "Lots of quick cuts, you know? A really cool music track. Maybe Beck. Just like a really interesting documentary, you know?"

I *didn't* know. And the incessant filming was getting on my nerves.

"Okay," Lindsay said. "If you don't care about our school project, we'll just sit here quietly."

"Of course we care about your school project," Megan said, taking a deep breath. "But your father and I are working now. You know how important *our* project is."

"So we can't just sit here quietly?" Alex asked.

"Why would you even want to?" I asked.

Both Alex and Lindsay still had their standard New Burg smiles, but when Lindsay replied, there was a definite edge to her voice.

"Yeah. You're right. Why would we want to?"

She turned to Alex. "Let's go," she said.

And they disappeared out the door.

"Were we too harsh?" Megan said.

"No," I said. "It's unnerving—this sudden interest the kids have in hanging out with us."

"Maybe it's just a sign that they're growing up. They want to be with us."

"I never wanted to be with *my* parents," I said.

Megan said, "I'm not surprised. I've met your parents."

"Now, *that's* harsh."

"They just like to hang out with us. Is that so terrible?"

"I don't know," I said. "It seems that a lot of the time they spend with us they're not exactly...interacting. They don't talk very much. When we're online, when we're reading. They even come up to the office and..." I struggled for the words.

Megan said, "And hang out."

"No, not just hang out. Watch us. I feel like they're watching us."

She laughed. Then she leaned in and kissed me.

"The only things watching us," Megan said, "are the drones and the surveillance cameras."

"And now the drones and the surveillance cameras are watching our children watching us. Look. I'm worried. Sure, they love school. They love their friends and their teachers and . . . well, here's the thing. This project is a perfect example. They are so intense about it, so into it . . . it's like they're turning into . . . I don't know. They're just not the Alex and Lindsay I know."

"I understand, but it was bound to happen," Megan said.

"That they'd become strangers?"

"No. That they'd grow up."

We both returned to our laptops. But not for long. There was a knock, and suddenly Alex appeared in our workroom.

"Oh, honey," Megan said nicely. "No more video. Please."

"No," he said. "No more video. But there's something I've been wanting to say to you both." The smile was still on his face. So how bad could it be?

"Go ahead," I said.

"This book you two are doing . . ."

"What about it?" Megan asked.

"Stop it. Stop doing it. Stop writing it."

"Why?" I asked.

"Please, just stop it," he said.

And again I asked, "But why?"

"It's a *bad idea.*"

The ever-present smile suddenly and completely left his face. Alex walked to the door. Then he turned and spoke one final time.

"*A really bad idea.*"

CHAPTER 31

ON MONDAY morning Megan's boss, Sam Reed (known to Megan and me as Sam Slimeball), informed Megan that he and she would be attending a five-day conference for Store supervisors. It would be held at the main office, in San Francisco.

On Monday night I dreamed that Megan and Sam Reed were standing naked in the fulfillment center, loading a two-thousand-count carton of Trojan Ultra Ribbed lubricated latex condoms onto a Stormer that I was driving.

Okay, I know it was a fairly sick and predictable dream, but the next morning I told Megan that it might be a great idea if I tagged along on the San Francisco trip. After all, workers who had just started at the Store were automatically entitled to five vacation days.

"Don't waste your vacation time, Jacob. What's more, you're patronizing me. I'm no little girl. I can take care of myself."

"Look, we both know he's going to try to jump you when you two are away together," I said.

"Yeah, I'm sure he'll try to pull some shit. But I've put him in his place before, and I'll do it again...and again...and again."

"C'mon. I'll buy myself a cheap ticket and go. Maybe between the two of us we can get some really hot info for the book. Just tell Slimeball that I'm coming. I won't be in the way. Tell him we've never been to San Francisco, and we always wanted to climb Nob Hill."

"Well, first of all, that's a lie. We *have* been to San Francisco," she said.

"Big deal. Twenty years ago, when we were barely out of college and totally broke," I said. "Camping out in Golden Gate Park, eating lunch at soup kitchens, walking—"

Megan cut me off before I really started to stroll down memory lane.

"Okay. Much as I hate lying, I can live with that lie. But I know Sam's going to have a shit fit when I tell him you're joining us."

"Good. That makes me feel even better about going."

Megan turned out to be absolutely right about Sam Slimeball's reaction. He was pissed and disappointed and tried like hell to dissuade her. He said point-blank that this was an "opportunity" for him and Megan to really get to know each other.

Megan told me that she said, "That's exactly what I was afraid of: you want to really get to know me better."

Her response to Sam Reed's comment sounded a little

too aggressive to believe, even for a strong woman like Megan.

But what the hell. Like I said, Megan wasn't lying. If that's what she said she said...then that's what she said.

I sure hoped I was right about that.

CHAPTER 32

IT TURNED out that Megan and Sam were booked on a separate charter flight with a big group of executive-level people from the Store. That group was flying out of Omaha, the airport where my family and I landed when we first arrived here.

Me? I was leaving two hours later from NBU—the airport code for New Burg, Nebraska.

If you accidentally happened upon New Burg International Airport, or—amazingly—had to fly out of the place, you'd think it was just another sleepy Midwest airport, home to a few business flights, a few private planes, some commuter flights, and a handful of crop dusters. If you ignored the two jet runways all you'd see is a smallish ramshackle wooden terminal. Like most everything in New Burg, the building is quaint and small and designed to be cute—in this case, sporting gray weathered shingles and storm fencing around a parking lot that could accommodate only around a dozen cars.

But like almost everything in New Burg, looks usually prove to be wildly deceiving.

I parked and removed my suitcase from the trunk. It is one of my really stupid affectations that I refuse to use a suitcase with wheels. Every time Megan and I are at an airport, whether it's Rio or London or New York, she never tires of pointing out the many men younger than I am who are easily rolling a wheeled suitcase.

The doorway to the simple wooden terminal was not automatic. It actually had a doorknob. I turned it. I walked inside, and a woman dressed in a red skirt and a blue blazer, a woman who looked like she might have stepped out of a 1950s television commercial, greeted me.

"Welcome to NBU, sir. May I see your boarding pass?" she said. She was neither sweet nor sour. She was perfectly New Burg polite.

I showed her the boarding pass. After she examined it she handed it back and gestured to a closed door behind her.

"Use this escalator here, sir," she said. This door *did* open automatically. I stepped aboard the escalator, and I swiftly descended. Within moments I was in the most elaborate modern room I'd ever entered. It had things you'd find in other airports—moving sidewalks, flashing arrival and departure signs, steel desks that seemed to signal airline gates—but the sidewalks were faster, the signs brighter, the steel desks taller.

Everything seemed bigger than normal, better than normal. The walkways were wider. The domelike ceilings were higher.

I looked at the departure board, yet I saw nothing that indicated flights to San Francisco. No SFO. Lots of LGAs and JFKs and LAXs. But nothing to help me. The suitcase was beginning to feel heavier.

Then a woman—attractive, young, not wearing a uniform—approached me.

"Mr. Brandeis? Jacob Brandeis?" she asked.

"Yes, that's me."

"Wonderful."

"Yeah, it is wonderful," I said with a smile. She ignored my joke. I was beginning to realize that almost everyone in New Burg ignored my jokes. Maybe I just wasn't very funny.

She was holding a small electronic device. She looked down at it and then spoke.

"I see you're scheduled for the next flight to San Francisco. And that your wife left approximately two hours ago on a United flight from Omaha. And that you are traveling with two children," she said.

"Well, you're sort of right. My wife is traveling with a different group. But I was booked here by the Store."

"Right," she said, as if I had just told her that the sky was blue or the sun was hot.

"But you're scheduled to fly with two children, Alexander and Lindsay Anne."

"Yes. They're our children. But they're at home. They're in school," I said.

I was becoming nervous but not panicked-nervous. I was also noticing that almost every other person or group of people in the airport was being interviewed by a similarly attractive young woman using a handheld device. The only difference was that these other people seemed happy, almost giddy, in their conversations.

"Well," she said. "There has been some sort of mix-up. Let me try to straighten it out."

She punched some buttons.

Then she confirmed what she'd previously told me.

"No. The children should be with you. They must have Store child care and Store nutritional catering. They cannot be left alone."

"You see," I said, "they're old enough to be left alone. We've left them alone many times. They're perfectly capable. . . . The girl is—"

I was preparing myself for a big-time run-in with this woman. Suddenly she spoke, this time with a ridiculously wide grin.

"No problem, Jacob. No problem."

She then hit a few more keys on her handheld and continued speaking.

"Child-Care Look-In Assistance has been contacted, and both morning and evening meals have been arranged for nutritional standardization and accurate drone delivery."

All I could get out of my mouth was "Good. That's good."

"Gate 11," she said with that damned stupid smile. "Your San Francisco flight leaves in forty-five minutes. Enjoy."

Then she added, "Be at peace."

"By the way," I said. "What's the airline I'm flying?"

She smiled. Then she spoke.

"As I said, Mr. Brandeis. Be at peace."

CHAPTER 33

A LOT of things about San Francisco were unchanged since our visit twenty years ago. The charming cable cars still struggled up the hills, and the Golden Gate Bridge remained awesomely beautiful in its strange industrial orange paint.

Yet many other things had changed enormously. It wasn't just the hundreds of new forty-story buildings scraping the heavens or all those Silicon Valley billionaires jamming up the traffic with their Porsches and Mercedes.

One group of changes was particularly frightening to Megan and me. It was as if the little town of New Burg had been exploded into a giant chic city.

Government-placed CCTV cameras and Store-placed surveillance cameras were posted everywhere: on top of traffic lights and building entrances, on the refrigerated cases in delis, hidden in the stained-glass windows of Saint Mary's Cathedral, even on the doors of the bathroom stalls in AT&T Park.

Miniature audio pickups dotted every coffee-shop

table and every department-store counter and every hotel room. There were audio recorders in the taxis, the buses, the cable cars. There were cameras in the restaurants, the parks, the ferry to Alcatraz. Lots of people wore surgical masks, not merely because of the filthy air, I thought, but also because it helped hide their identities.

Just as depressing and creepy were the heavens above. That sunless sky was no longer just the result of the notorious San Francisco fog. No, the skies were also dark because they were thick with surveillance drones and delivery drones and research drones. The new San Francisco made me very scared, but it also made me very sad. I had seen the future, and it clearly belonged to the Store.

And oh, yes. One other thing had changed during this trip, and that other thing had nothing to do with San Francisco. It had everything to do with our obnoxious boss, Sam Reed.

Sam Reed, the same guy who couldn't keep his hands off my wife, the same guy who spoke to me as if I were a mongrel, had suddenly turned into my best bud. For no apparent reason.

"Hey, Jacob, I scored some tickets for the Giants-Dodgers game tonight. How about Megan does some shopping at Gump's and takes in a museum or two while we do the game? Then we can all meet up for a late dinner." Huh?

Here's another equally creepy and unexpected burst of humanity from Sam:

"Look, Jacob, I can't invite you to join Megan and me for tomorrow morning's lectures and meetings, but I can hook you in to the afternoon trip to Napa that they planned for us."

Both Megan and I were super suspicious, to say the least—Mr. Hyde was morphing into Dr. Jekyll way too easily.

Back at the Fairmont, where I was changing for our ball game, we discussed "the new Sam Reed."

As always, Megan didn't care that the surveillance cameras were recording our every word. She let fly with her opinion.

"He's up to something," Megan said. "There's no way someone like Sam can turn into Mr. Nice Guy overnight."

"Let's not push the Cynical button so fast," I said. "Maybe he's just sort of getting to know us, and he thinks, like, we're funny and smart and decent and—"

"Don't kid yourself, Jacob," Megan said. "Remember when we asked him about Bette and Bud yesterday? He just click-clacked his iPad, and in about ten seconds he said, 'Nope. Just transferred. Not here for a debriefing. Never were.'"

"Maybe that's all the info he got."

"Oh, come on. His voice turned to ice. His Mr. Nice Guy act totally folded. I think he was genuinely happy telling us that Bette and Bud were nowhere to be found. Think whatever you want," she added. "But I don't trust him one teensy little bit."

"I guess you're right," I said. "But we might as well enjoy the new Sam while we can. You know, before the old Sam reappears."

"You enjoy him," she said. "I'm not moving in too close."

I slipped into my jeans, and Megan pinned her hair on top of her head. As she dabbed on some eye makeup and pulled a fairly snug navy-blue T-shirt over her head, I couldn't help but think about her and Sam.

We both certainly knew him as a first-class sleazeball, but wasn't it just possible that he had settled down? Megan wasn't buying it "one teensy little bit." I sure didn't like the guy, but Megan actually hatcd him.

Or at least that's what she wanted me to think.

CHAPTER 34

THE MOST important event of the San Francisco conference was a totally mind-boggling surprise—a presentation by Thomas P. Owens, founder of the Store.

The fact was that nobody in the organization really knew Mr. Owens. Everyone seemed to believe he was in seclusion. One source said he was on a ranch in Brazil. Another said he had a twenty-room penthouse in Sardinia. We investigated every lead, and everything led to a dead end. Almost no one had ever met the guy.

Because of our secret book, Megan and I had some pretty hefty files on Owens. But even after we read all the information we had accumulated, even after we analyzed every business article about him, even after we tracked down and briefly interviewed a woman who claimed to be his illegitimate daughter, we knew just as little about Owens as everyone else did. Whether he was hiding behind a curtain somewhere in New York, in his hometown of Lorain, Ohio, or in the Land of Oz itself, nobody seemed to know. Yet everyone seemed to care.

I had no business being at Gallery 16, the terminally hip modern art gallery and exhibition hall where Thomas P. Owens was to appear. But I lucked out.

My new best friend, Sam Reed, had arranged for me to attend. A young doctor (at least I think he was a doctor) came to our room and administered an injection into my left elbow. He told me that the injection registered on a supersurveillance board and would allow me three-hour clearance and access to the event. Sam told me that this was standard procedure for admission to Owens's appearances.

When Sam, Megan, and I arrived at Gallery 16, Sam suggested, "You make yourself semi-scarce. You know, stand in the back with a few other illegal interlopers." Both Megan and Sam laughed a bit, but I obeyed. I made myself semi-scarce with a bunch of waiters and Store photographers standing on the sidelines. Meanwhile Sam and Megan were in the high-class seats—first row, on the aisle.

From where I was standing I had an excellent view of the eighty or so management members who filled the other seats. The men wore either blue blazers or dark suits. The women wore either dark slacks or modest dark dresses.

But the conservative clothes and the traditional New Burg smiles (even Megan had pasted a smile onto her face) could not disguise the fact that the room was electric with excitement. People were embracing. Some looked on the verge of tears. Everyone was talking excitedly. There is really only one way to describe it: this crowd was waiting for the Messiah.

Finally a woman walked to the front of the room. She stood directly in front of an Andy Warhol blue *Queen Elizabeth II* print. The audience became completely silent. The woman turned toward the audience and flashed the New Burg smile. I quickly recognized her as the woman who had presided over the disastrous Dr. David Werner lecture. She was apparently the official hostess for all off-site meetings at the Store.

I could not resist speaking to the female stranger standing next to me.

"That woman is wearing an Isabel Toledo dress," I said.

"Oh, good," she said, then she moved a few inches away from me.

The onstage woman spoke: "I must say that I share your exhilaration and anticipation at this very rare opportunity to meet and greet the Store's founder and conscience, Mr. Thomas P. Owens."

The applause was wildly enthusiastic.

"As such, you can imagine that I then share your deep disappointment in learning just a few minutes ago that Mr. Owens will not be able to join us this afternoon."

The moans, the shout-outs of "What?" "Why not?" "What happened?"

"Mr. Owens sends his deepest apologies and his warmest wishes for a fruitful and invigorating conference in the Bay Area. Please enjoy the beverages at the various bars, and don't miss the omelet and crepe station and the blini and caviar station."

The hostess walked away and into the groups of people that were forming around the room. The New Burg smiles

146

had all but disappeared. Some people held one another. Others bowed their heads. A handful of them were dabbing at their eyes; they were actually weeping. Is this what happens when you're expecting the Messiah and he fails to show up?

I almost could not believe what I was seeing, and when I glanced toward the first row I truly could not believe what I was seeing. Megan and Sam.

What the hell was happening? Megan was crying. I also saw that Sam Reed had his arms around her. Apparently he was trying to comfort her.

Sure.

CHAPTER 35

I DIDN'T have time to be pissed off about the warm hug Sam had just wrapped around Megan.

No. I had something much bigger to be pissed off about: Megan and I had been summoned for "an in-depth interview and analysis" at the Store headquarters.

"It's no big deal," Sam told us. "They knew Megan was here, and of course they found out immediately that you had come along, Jacob. So it looked to the senior interview committee like perfect timing."

"But they asked us every conceivable question in the world when they interviewed us back in New Burg," Megan said. "Does everyone get this interview treatment? Or is it just those of us who might be a little out of control?"

"Not *everybody* has this interview. There's no pattern to who gets it. It's kinda random," Sam said. "Look. It's only around an hour, and everyone's really nice, and it's just for their records, and—"

"And I guess we can't say we won't do it," I said.

The stern, nasty voice of the "real" Sam Reed returned.

"I wouldn't recommend it."

So that afternoon Megan and I sat in a very large, very stark conference room containing nothing but four comfortable leather chairs and a small glass coffee table on top of which sat a silver pitcher of coffee, another of tea, and four bottles of mineral water.

Our interviewers were a man and a woman. Like everyone employed by the Store, they were unfailingly polite and friendly, but they did not offer their names when we shook hands. The two of them looked like they were in their twenties. They looked more like graduate students, and in fact I wondered if Megan and I were so unimportant in the great scheme of the Store that we were just practice interviewees for these "kids."

The woman said, "Let's begin. But I should mention that you may find the first few questions a bit...shall we say...obvious or ridiculous." Then she read from her laptop.

"From the following list, select the group you would most likely want to be part of: A, the Church of Scientology; B, the Ku Klux Klan; C, the Store."

"Before I struggle to answer, let me just say you were almost right," I said. "The questions are...shall we say... obvious *and* ridiculous."

"Well," the young man said, "wait till you hear the next one." Then he read from his laptop.

"Of the many wonderful foods available at the various markets and delivery services in New Burg, what would you say is your family's favorite?"

It didn't take a degree in psychology to realize that

the whole "ridiculous" conversation was meant to disarm Megan and me, turn the interviewers and the interviewees into old friends. So the four of us chuckled along for a few minutes.

But within five minutes, the nature of the questions began to change.

"So a writer like you, Jacob, can't be very satisfied gathering products down at the fulfillment center. You must be doing some writing in your spare time."

I had barely given my evasive, bullshitty response when the woman interviewer asked: "What private writing project are you working on now, Jacob? Something personal? Something autobiographical? Something about your employer? You can be honest with us."

Yeah. Sure. I would cut off my hands at the wrists rather than tell them the truth. So I said, "I am writing, but it's nothing important, nothing that's really come together. In a way it's autobiographical. I'll let you know as I get a little further into it."

With her smile in place, the young woman said, "I'm sure you will. That'd be great."

The young man leaned in toward us with that phony-looking concern usually found in insurance salesmen and annoying uncles.

"The children—Alex and Lindsay. How are they adjusting to their new environment?"

"Really well. They love school. They've made friends," Megan said.

"Yeah. The kids are probably doing better than Megan and I are."

The two interviewers looked unpleasantly or pleasantly surprised (it was hard to tell those two expressions apart in New Burg). Megan shot me a look that more or less meant, "Don't be such an asshole."

The young man got us back on track immediately.

"I understand that Alex is pretty much the star of the junior boxing team."

Alex? Boxing? The star? The only sport Alex was ever interested in is played on a big soft sofa. The equipment is an electronic device, and that device is attached to a television monitor.

"In the spirit of honesty," I said. "Alex's boxing is complete news to me. Did he tell you about this, Megan?"

"Oh, he may have mentioned it once. I'm not sure," she said. As I said, she was not a good liar.

Then the young woman spoke.

"Perhaps he kept this information from you, Mr. Brandeis, because he knows of your abhorrence of rough contact sports like boxing and football."

"I've never discussed that subject with Alex."

"But my statement does correctly reflect your beliefs. You are opposed to boxing in principle."

"Well, yes. But I've never discussed that with Alex or anyone else. I mean, it's a belief, not . . . I don't know . . . not an obsession or a cause or a passion or . . ."

"If we could, let's return briefly to another subject. Mrs. Brandeis, do you assist your husband on the book he's writing?"

I stood up. And I was furious.

"What the hell are you talking about—'the book your

husband is writing'? I just told you that I have some thoughts about writing a book. I'm not actually writing a book! I gotta tell you, I don't even know what the purpose of this interview is. I realize that with all your cameras and spies and shit you know a lot about what we do. But this is all crazy. Absolutely crazy."

The woman suggested we take a break, and I stupidly realized, belatedly, that the two mirrors against the mostly bare walls of the room were most likely two-way, that we were being watched during the interview.

"No. We don't need a break. Because we don't need an interview," I said.

"Jacob, please. Let's try to cooperate," Megan said, and frankly I couldn't believe she was saying it.

Then the young man spoke.

"We really don't have much more to cover—a few questions about a police raid at a house party you attended, and then—"

"The interview is absolutely over," I said. Now I was screaming. "We're leaving."

Megan was still seated. I glared at her. She slowly stood up and picked up her pocketbook from the floor.

"Do whatever you want with us," I said. "Transfer us. Put us in jail. Shoot us. Whatever. We are out of here."

CHAPTER 36

MEGAN HAS two kinds of anger: anger that screams and anger that doesn't speak a word. There was no predicting which one was going to erupt. I had guessed that after my behavior at the interview there would be a lot of shouting and swearing and declarations of "I don't care if I'm making a scene." As is often the case, I turned out to be wrong. Dead wrong.

Megan was completely silent as we walked back to the hotel. That's precisely the kind of anger I didn't want. I wanted her to scream at me and tell me how stupidly I had acted at the "interview." I wanted her to get it out of her system, and by doing that to force me back into the frightening world of the Store.

"Okay, okay," I said, trying to force some reaction from her. "I was a complete fool. I should have listened and answered and played along."

She said nothing.

"I know our whole future depends on writing this book. I know I've seriously jeopardized it. I know I behaved like an idiot. And I know you have every right in the world to be pissed off at me."

Still nothing.

The very normal creepiness of the San Francisco streets only made things worse. This was a big, beautiful city version of New Burg: the drones clogging the sky, one of them clearly assigned to Megan and me; it moved like a big electronic umbrella over our heads. Then there were the tiny video cameras embedded in building walls and stop signs and the rims of trash cans. The trash cans themselves were models of Store efficiency: drop a piece of paper or plastic into the mouth of the garbage container, and the item was silently sucked into a below-ground recycling system.

It was all perfect and neat and scary as shit...at least to me.

Suddenly Megan stopped walking. Her head was bowed. I stopped also.

"Listen to me, Jacob. This is important for you to understand. I'm *not* angry at you. I love you. But it feels like you've just gone over the edge. And I understand that. This new world, this new place, these new rules...they're very hard on you. But your behavior makes things impossible for the rest of us—for Lindsay and Alex...and for me."

"But it was so outrageous what they were doing in that interview room," I began.

"Yes. Yes. It was outrageous. I know that, and you know that. But this sudden inability you've developed—the fact that you simply can't hold your temper inside you for . . . for . . . well, the only way I know how to put it is 'for the greater good'—has become kind of a problem. I'm worried."

"Don't worry," I said. "I know that everything will—"

"Turn out all right? No. You don't know that at all." Couples who are really invested in being couples can always finish each other's sentences.

Megan kept talking. "I'm worried about what you've turned into. We're all *on* the edge. But I think you may have gone *over* the edge."

I put my arms on her shoulders. I moved in a step to hold her, hug her. She began to cry. Nothing big, just short little bursts of sobs.

Shit! Was there any truth in what Megan was thinking and feeling and saying? Was I becoming a strange new person in this strange new world? Yeah, for sure I hated this insanity of complete automation—no books, no pens, no humans manning the trolleys and trains. I was not adapting. I was still always reaching for paper money to pay for things, yet in this new world only cards and cell phones tendered valid currency. I missed everything about my old life. I wanted to watch a crappy Knicks game on a TV set, not see the game on some handheld interactive screen. I wanted to go to the supermarket and squeeze the honeydew melons and get suckered into buying cereal we didn't need. I didn't want to push some buttons and have our pantry reload automatically.

Even as I held Megan close, I looked around and could not feel calm. There were so many people on the street wearing masks and earphones and environmental-protection jumpsuits. The very air had a perpetual scent of a combination of rubber and ammonia as well as just a touch of something floral. I called it gardenia vomit.

Megan looked up and smiled at me. "Gardenia vomit getting to you?" she said. Then we continued to walk.

"Christ," I said. "I hope I haven't screwed things up for us."

I was hoping Megan would say something like "Of course not. Everything will be okay."

But she said nothing. We kept walking.

We were at the hotel now. The drone that was trailing us drifted skyward. In-hotel devices would be taking over our surveillance.

The doorman opened the door and spoke cordially. "Welcome back, Mr. and Mrs. Brandeis. There are two people waiting for you in the lobby."

CHAPTER 37

"HEY, BRANDEISES! Over here!"

It was a woman's voice, happy and loud.

"Look to your right. We're over here," shouted a man.

Megan's own voice suddenly changed to little-girl wonder.

"Oh, my God! It's Bette and Bud!" she shouted.

Oh, my God. It *was* Bette and Bud. They both looked a little younger, a little thinner, a little...well, a little "cooler" than they did back in New Burg.

We hugged. We kissed. We did that thing you do when you hold a person at arm's length and then lean back and look at him or her from head to toe. Bette, Bud, and I sat on a sofa; Megan sat on a big club chair.

"You guys look terrific," I said. And I meant it. It felt like six months since they'd left New Burg, and now they were looking around ten years younger.

"You really do look terrific," Megan said. Since Megan was the thoughtful brains of our outfit, she added, "I mean, you always looked good, but you've both lost weight, and Bette's haircut is *très* chic, and…I dunno… everything. Like, your skin is healthy, and these clothes are all Ralph Laureny."

I guess she finally ran out of compliments to hand out. Megan turned silent but kept on smiling. It should have been a perfect time for Bette and Bud to tell us how terrific we both looked.

"Well, Megan looks as beautiful as ever," Bette said.

"She certainly does. Looks even younger than when we last saw each other," Bud added.

Uh-huh, I was thinking. *Keep going, folks. Tell me how great I look.*

Instead Bud smiled and said, "Now, you, on the other hand, Jacob, look like you've been working too hard. Are they working you too hard?" He chuckled.

"No. Hard but not too hard," I said.

"And he's lost about ten pounds since the last time you saw him," chimed in Megan. "Without trying to lose it."

"What? Are you three ganging up on me? Maybe I need a makeover."

I laughed, but nobody else laughed. I was pissed off, but nobody seemed to notice.

"Listen, Jacob," said Bette. "I'm a big proponent of watching your weight, but too thin is just as bad as too fat."

Megan said "Amen." I looked at her with that what-the-hell-is-going-on-here look. She smiled and said, "It's all for your own good."

I was thinking that whenever someone said that something was for your own good, it never really was. But even more, I was thinking how hurt and angry I was that Megan jumped on the "Doesn't Jacob look like shit" band-wagon.

Fortunately a waiter came to take a drink order (on his electronic pad, of course; I think I was the last person in America who still used an old-fashioned lead pencil).

Megan asked for a vodka and tonic. Bette ordered Diet Coke. Bud ordered club soda ("and don't go putting any lime twist in it, ya hear?"). I ordered a Chivas on the rocks.

"You guys on the wagon?" I asked.

"Not really," Bette said. "We're just trying to cut back. That's always good advice."

I wondered why she felt she needed to call what she said good advice.

Megan then told them that we had tried to locate them when we'd arrived in San Francisco.

"Well, we didn't come to San Francisco when we *first* got transferred," Bette said. "They sent us to San Diego."

"San Jose," Bud corrected her.

"Oh, all these saints," Bette said. "Clara, Monica, Anita, Diego, Clemente. I can't remember where I am half the time."

"So tell us," Megan said. "What are you doing here? It seems like you just disappeared from New Burg overnight."

"Well, we *did* leave New Burg overnight," Bette said. "Some exec at the Store called and said they'd send a car to take us to the airport and have a private company plane at the airport to whisk us away to . . ." She hesitated for a moment. "San Jose.

"So that's where we're living and working. Only about an hour from here. I'm at the fulfillment center in San Mateo.... There ya go, another saint's name," she added.

Bette and Bud looked at each other with bright eyes and broad smiles. In fact it seemed like they hadn't stopped smiling since the moment we'd spotted them.

I should have dropped the subject. I tried, but I couldn't.

"Look. We're your friends. You were our best friends in New Burg. Tell us what happened," I said, perhaps a bit too intensely.

"What happened, Jacob, is what we told you," said Bud, the smile gone from his face. "They called. They said they wanted us to get ready. The plane was ready. So *we* got ready. And we got transferred."

I was becoming very impatient. My voice shot up pretty loudly.

"Who the hell is 'they'? Who is the 'they' that called? And why did it have to be overnight, immediately? And what exactly does it mean to be transferred? Answer me. Tell me. You two just disappeared. That's not normal! That's not natural!"

"Calm down, Jacob," Megan said.

Bette spoke. "It seemed perfectly natural to us."

"It's not!" I shouted. "It's not perfectly natural to be flown off in the middle of the night to a new place. That's not how things happen in this world."

There was a long pause. I took a big gulp of my Scotch. Then Bud spoke.

"That's exactly how things happen in *this* world. And if

for some reason it doesn't seem perfectly natural to you, that's fine. But it does seem perfectly natural to us."

The Refill button on the coffee table in front of us was flashing. We all ignored it, and the flashing eventually stopped.

Bette tried to restore order. Her sweet little voice came into the conversation as if nothing unpleasant or argumentative had been said.

"So," she said. "That's how the transfer happened. A private plane, a zip-zip-zip out to San Jose."

"All in a few hours?" Megan asked. "That's amazing."

"Actually, it's kinda creepy," I said. Megan reached out and patted my hand gently. I was becoming an expert at saying the wrong thing. And Megan was becoming an expert at bailing me out.

"I don't think it's creepy," Megan said. "I think it actually sounds kinda cool."

"And that plane ride sure was luxurious. Just six seats on the plane, a full kitchen, a bar…" Bud began rattling on.

"Pipe down, Bud," Bette said with a chuckle. "I'm sure the Brandeises have been on a private plane."

"Well, if you think that, then you'd be wrong," I said. Bette and Bud laughed so hard you'd have thought Joan Rivers had left me that punch line in her will.

The laughter stopped. But our old friends never stopped smiling. The anger and cynicism they had both harbored about the Store seemed to have completely evaporated. Here they were in their cool clothes and their smiley faces, happy in their jobs and happy in their lives.

We finished our drinks.

I did ask them how they knew Megan and I were in San Francisco.

Bud casually replied, "Oh, you guys know how everyone in the Store knows everything about everyone else."

"That's part of the charm of it," Megan said.

"Yeah. A big part of the charm," I added.

I don't think either Bette or Bud knew for sure whether I was being sarcastic or not.

We chatted for a while about our kids, their new house, Bette's new haircut. Then it was time to say good-bye.

We all stood up and said how great it was to catch up. It felt like old times. Bette and Megan hugged each other. Bud hugged Megan. Then, just before we went our separate ways, Bud turned and gave me an unexpected hug as well.

"Don't forget," he whispered in my ear. "You never know for sure whether you can trust us."

CHAPTER 38

MEGAN AND I watched Bette and Bud leave. We sat silently in the lobby. After a few minutes I said, "I'm sorry, sweetie. I'll be better. I'll control myself." Then I made those little quotation marks with my fingers and said, "I'll get with 'the program.'"

Megan nodded gently.

Nighttime had sneaked up on us. It was eight o'clock, and I was hungry.

"You want to go get some food? We haven't had anything since breakfast."

"Sure," Megan said. It was not a good, solid "Sure," but it was a yes nonetheless.

"Should we text Sam and see if he wants to join us?" I asked.

"No," she said. "There's some important meeting of big shots that he has to go to. We're on our own."

After consulting the concierge, we headed south to the Nob Hill Café. "Nearby and reasonable," he had said. "You've sure got our profile," I had answered.

"Yes, I do," said the concierge, and I realized he wasn't joking.

The night had that chill that everyone says is special to San Francisco. So we walked quickly.

It was the usual crowd: tourists, natives, people in surgical masks, drones overhead, and, of course, our personal drone hovering over Megan and me. Megan never seemed to mind the surveillance. It always made me furious.

As one of the WALK signs changed to DON'T WALK, I said, "Let's go. We can beat this light."

"No," she said. "I hate it when you cross against the light."

"C'mon. I'm cold."

We started to cross. Our drone was keeping up with us. It swooped in low, very low, almost hitting us.

Immediately there was the sound of a car horn. We saw a huge SUV, a Chevy Tahoe, a foot or two away from us. We managed to stop short and avoid it. The low-flying drone was not so lucky. The drone slammed mercilessly into the driver's side of the SUV. The crash was deafening. The crash was hideous. The Tahoe crumbled into a broken smashed mess of steel. Immediately fire began raging under the hood of the vehicle. People gathered around the crash; others ran from the blaze. The fire spread almost instantly throughout the rest of the Tahoe. The battered and squashed drone was trapped in the rear part of the SUV, snug against the disfigured, bloody faces of two small children. The two kids in the back and what looked like the mom and dad in the front burned like fireplace logs, as if gasoline had been poured on them, and then—*boom!*— they ignited.

Megan and I and four other people tried to get to the passengers, but the heat was unbearable, and it was clearly too late to help.

We heard distant sirens and a few crazy-sounding old-fashioned fire engine bells. As we watched, we realized to our horror that there was another child in the way-back section. That kid was also on fire.

A car marked SFPD arrived with three police officers inside. Then we heard an insistent, relentless beeping noise from above. Within a minute, two massive drones swept down to the scene of the accident. Each drone had mechanical claws dropping from its base down to the twisted, burning mess below. One drone clamped its claws onto the front of the SUV. The other drone performed the identical maneuver at the rear. Together they lifted the entire vehicle, including our personal drone—part of this awful piece of steel sculpture—into the dark city skies. It seemed like a strange mechanical ballet as the burning SUV was lifted up and up and up, looking from a distance like a flying piece of slowly dying charcoal.

The few people who remained on the scene watched until the SUV disappeared. The three policemen told people to move on.

I walked toward one of the cops.

"I saw this all happen, Officer. I was even sort of involved. Let me—" I said.

"Please move on, sir. It's over."

"Jacob, please. Let's go," Megan shouted.

"But—" I said.

Suddenly there were the sounds you usually hear when a truck backs up—that irritating *beep-beep-beep*. Sure enough, the sound was coming from two trucks, but they weren't backing up. They were driving straight down Mason Street very slowly. Each one looked like a very modernist marriage between a garbage truck and a sleek luxury bus. Big heavy steel scrapers—like enormous spatulas—were attached to their fronts. They gathered debris—scraps of metal, burned luggage, a Coca-Cola cooler—and then lifted it into construction bins attached to the trucks' sides.

Then it was over. Totally over.

The people dispersed. The streets were clean. The trucks drove away. Five people had died brutally, yet it was as if nothing had happened.

"I feel like I just stepped in and out of a nightmare," I said to Megan.

A lone policeman's voice: "I thought I told you folks to move along."

We weren't hungry anymore. We headed back to our hotel. A new drone—a replacement drone—was now assigned to follow us.

"That was fast," the concierge said. We said nothing.

Back in our rooms, we immediately turned on our computers. Local websites? Nothing. National websites? Nothing. AOL? CNN? Nothing. We turned on the television. TV news? Nothing.

The next morning the *San Francisco Chronicle* was delivered to our hotel room door. The Metro section? Nothing.

Nothing. Nothing. Nothing. As if the accident had never happened.

CHAPTER 39

"I HAVEN'T heard a word about it," Sam said.

Megan, Sam, and I were on our way to the San Francisco airport. The taxi driver had barely closed the car trunk when I asked Sam if he'd known about the SUV accident the night before. He didn't.

"That's unbelievable," I replied.

Megan gently but firmly disagreed with me.

"C'mon, Jacob. It was pretty awful, yes, but not *that* newsworthy. I mean, it wasn't 9/11," she said. I was fairly outraged that Sam laughed at Megan's uncharacteristically tasteless joke.

The check-in machines spat out our tickets, and when I looked at mine it said SPEED-CHECK. I assumed that we all were going to go through speed-check, but it appears I was alone in receiving this convenience.

"Well, aren't *you* special?" Sam said with another laugh, and I headed toward the speed-check area with—okay, I admit it—a slightly smug farewell: "See you at the gate," I said to Megan and her boss.

Good luck turned into bad luck in approximately five seconds. The moment I showed my boarding pass to the guard, he asked me to step aside and join him at "the desk." That desk turned out to be a small, cheap-looking card table parked in front of a metal door bearing the sign SECURITY: APPROVED PERSONNEL ONLY. A middle-aged woman wearing one of those uniforms that's supposed to remind you of the police smiled at me and then spoke.

"Were you in San Francisco for business or pleasure, Mr. Brandeis?"

"Uh, both."

"What type of business was it?" she asked.

"I work for the Store. They were having a national meeting."

She pushed a few buttons on her computer, scrolled down a few pages, and then spoke again.

"I don't have you listed at that meeting, sir. There's a Megan Brandeis on the—"

"She's my wife," I said. I glanced up and saw that Sam and Megan had already passed through "normal" security, but speed-check had me waiting. Then the security woman signaled to another agent, who was holding an electronic wand.

"If you don't mind, Mr. Brandeis, this officer is going to screen you electronically."

I did mind, of course, but this was no time to make a scene.

The wanding procedure took less than fifteen seconds.

"That's fine, Mr. Brandeis," the woman said. "Now we'd like to continue the screening privately. This officer from airport security would like you to accompany him through this door to an examination booth."

"What? Are you kidding me?" I said.

"No, sir. I am not. It's a normal procedure, for your own safety as well as everyone else's. Just through this door behind me," she said.

"But why?"

"It's just a procedure, sir. If you care to continue with boarding, please cooperate."

"But *why?*" I asked again.

"Sir, please," she said. By this time the other agent had opened the SECURITY door. Before I walked through the door I looked out toward the area where Megan and Sam had been standing. After a few seconds I spotted them. Sam was talking on his cell phone. Megan was talking on hers.

The agent holding the door open spoke for the first time.

"We're losing patience, sir. Please come with me."

CHAPTER 40

SWEATING. PANTING. Dry-mouthed. That was me, the last passenger to board United Airlines flight 5217 from SFO to Omaha.

My boarding pass was clenched between my teeth. My shirttail was flying like a miniskirt over my chinos. And I only hoped to God that I had remembered to put my laptop back in my carry-on after the twenty-minute security check.

Immediately I ran into my traveling companions, Megan and Sam . . . in first class. To add insult to injury, they were both sipping Champagne.

"We thought you missed the flight, man," Sam said. "We were worried."

I couldn't figure out whether he actually *was* worried or whether he simply was trying to *sound* worried.

"What happened, Jacob?" Megan asked. She probably thought that I had done something to cause the delay.

A flight attendant behind me said, "We're ready for takeoff, sir. Please take your seat."

"Yes, ma'am," I said. I guess I was getting used to taking orders.

"I upgraded Megan and me to first class," Sam said. "But we'll trade seats. You sit here with your wife. I don't mind flying in the back." Before I could protest his generous gesture he had grabbed my boarding pass and headed through the curtains to the back. I settled in next to Megan, and we both remained silent throughout the safety instruction video.

Megan broke the silence only seconds after "...and we do hope you enjoy the flight."

"Jacob," she said. "I was worried about you. So was Sam."

"Well, you couldn't have been *that* worried. I saw you two on your cell phones," I said, sounding a lot like a six-year-old.

"We just assumed you had gone to the men's room or gone to pick up a sandwich or something. Oh, Jacob," she said, her eyes full of concern and her hands reaching to touch my shoulder and arm. "I feel terrible. What happened?"

I was about to tell her when a voice came through the loudspeaker.

"This is your captain, Brian Heller. Before takeoff we have some final luggage checking to take care of. It shouldn't take more than a few minutes. Then we'll be off to lovely Omaha, where the temperature is...sixty-three degrees. Thanks for your patience."

Almost immediately, two flight attendants appeared at my seat.

"Mr. Brandeis?" the male attendant asked.

"Yes."

"I understand that this is not your originally assigned seat."

More grief, I assumed.

"Well, a friend of mine gave me his—"

"Yes," the woman attendant said. "No problem, Mr. Brandeis. However, the captain…" There was a pause. Then the male flight attendant chimed in.

"The captain would like to examine your carry-on luggage, sir. Is this backpack the only luggage you brought aboard?" he asked as he lifted the backpack resting on my lap.

"Well, yeah. But why does he need—I mean, I've never had this happen before."

"Please, sir," said the attendant.

"Jacob, please, just do it. I'm sure it's nothing," said Megan.

The two flight attendants took the backpack, and they brought it through the open cockpit door.

"I'm going to see what's going on," I said to Megan, and I started to unbuckle my seat belt.

"Just stay put," Megan said. She spoke firmly. She seemed amazingly calm herself.

Within a few minutes, the male flight attendant returned with the backpack.

"Thank you for your cooperation, sir. No problem," he said.

"What were you looking for?" I asked with a touch of impatience.

"Just a precaution, sir. Thank you. Can I get you some Champagne or fresh-squeezed orange juice, sir, when we reach our cruising altitude?"

"No, thank you," I said.

Captain Heller's voice again: "Flight attendants, please prepare for takeoff."

The plane taxied down the runway, and we were off.

"Tell me what happened in that speed-check place," Megan said.

"You and Sam saw it," I began.

"No, we didn't. We didn't know anything was wrong."

"Okay, okay," I said. "They took me off the line. They brought me into a special room, and two guys searched me. It was…forget it. The details are kinda gross."

"Gross?" she said. "What happened?"

"I had to strip down to my underwear. So I stood there, practically naked, and they wanded me…everywhere— my ears, my neck, my armpits, my crotch. They both had rubber gloves on, and one of them put his hand…"

I paused. For some reason I felt like I was about to cry.

"Oh, forget it," I said. "You can imagine the rest."

"Oh, my God," she said. "That's horrible. No wonder you're so upset."

I closed my eyes and opened them about five minutes later. Megan had taken out her laptop and was busily tapping away at it. When I looked out the plane window I saw at least forty drones flying alongside the plane. They looked like huge black-and-gray birds in a formation flying south for the winter.

"Holy shit!" I said.

"What the matter?" Megan said.

"Out the window. Around a million drones."

Megan glanced out the window for a few seconds.

"Oh, Jacob, please. They're delivering merchandise."

I was silent for a few seconds. Then I turned and looked at her squarely, face-to-face, close in. I spoke.

"You think I'm crazy, don't you?"

There was only a momentary pause, but that moment felt like an hour.

"No. I don't think you're crazy. I think you're tired."

"But the drones—"

"Jacob. C'mon. Like I said. They're just delivery drones. There's nothing to be afraid of."

CHAPTER 41

SUITCASES, LAPTOP cases, carry-on luggage, shopping bags. Megan and I arrived through the back door and into our kitchen late that evening. Back home in good old New Burg.

Okay, Lindsay and Alex were way past the stage when they might welcome us yelling, "Yay! Mommy and Daddy are home!" when we returned from a trip. But the least they could do was come down and say hello. Instead our welcome-home greeting consisted of a shout from Alex in his room.

"Who the hell is downstairs?"

"It's us!" Megan shouted.

"Oh, hi," Alex yelled back.

I walked to the bottom of the hall staircase.

"Where's your sister?"

"How would I know?" Alex yelled.

I swore to myself that I wouldn't get angry.

"I'm up here," came Lindsay's voice. No hello. No welcome back. Just "I'm up here."

So much for swearing that I wouldn't get angry.

Megan joined me in the hall.

"Couldn't you guys come down and say hello?" she shouted up the stairs.

"In a few minutes" was Alex's answer. Lindsay's response was even worse: "Can't. Busy."

Megan shook her head and walked into the kitchen, but I didn't move, except to sit down on the bottom hall step. I used my hands to try to wipe the heavy perspiration from my face. It was not a particularly efficient method. Then I buried my wet face in my wet hands. The feeling I had on the plane returned, the feeling that I might at any moment burst into tears.

A sense of confusion. A kind of sadness that was mixed with anger. Megan's impatience. Bette and Bud's transformation into smiley faces. The SUV accident. The drones crowding every piece of sky that I walked under.

I stood up and climbed to the third step. And I screamed.

"Get down here right now. Right now! Do you hear me? Right now." I couldn't stop yelling. I couldn't stop the words from tumbling so fiercely out of my mouth.

"Are you hearing me? Are you two deaf? You two are wanted down here immediately!"

My daughter and son appeared.

They looked confused.

My arms and hands were shaking. My stomach tightened. My legs and head ached.

By now Megan had also appeared.

"What's wrong, Jacob?"

"What's wrong?" I bellowed. "Our kids couldn't even come downstairs and say hello to us. That's what's wrong."

Deadly silence.

"What's the big deal?" Alex said. But I did not have the energy to continue my rant.

"What's happening to you, Daddy?" Lindsay said.

Instead I said quietly, "Never mind. Just go back to whatever you were doing." They looked at me suspiciously. Then they turned and went back upstairs.

I looked at Megan. "I worry that we're losing the kids," I said.

"I worry that we're losing you," she said.

I thought I had spent all my anger and energy, but suddenly I could feel it building up again. The tension returned to my limbs. The throbbing returned to my head.

"Megan," I said. "I'm going upstairs to do some work on the book."

"Well, what about the luggage and dinner and checking e-mail and—" she was rattling away. I interrupted.

"No! Not now. Leave me alone. I'm going upstairs to do some work on the book. I'm fresh right now. I want to work now." I picked up my computer case and began running up the stairs, two steps at a time, three steps at a time. I was outside the workroom door. In my head I heard the umpire shout.

Safe at home!

CHAPTER 42

I PULLED open the attic workroom door with so much energy that a screw popped out of one of its hinges.

The workroom was totally overwhelming me with dry heat. I actually loved it. I loved that my eyes burned and my skin exploded with sweat. I pulled off my shirt like a fighter who was late for a match. I used my shirt to blot the sweat from my face and hair and neck.

I spread my notes—scrawled on scraps of paper, the backs of envelopes—across the dusty floor. I hadn't felt this excited in days. The anger within me had been replaced by an almost uncontrollable energy.

I zipped quickly through my computer notes, transferring important topics and facts onto the ever-growing pile of index cards. As the pencil lead wore out or broke, I'd grab a new one and keep going. I could not write fast enough.

I wasn't clear, but I think my plan was to get as much done as I could before Megan showed up to tell me that what I was doing was wrong. It wasn't too many hours away from tomorrow, when I'd once again be lifting gallons of apple juice and boxes of microwave ovens and cartons of hedge clippers and...

And then I had an idea that I knew was great. I also knew that if Megan had been there she would not have agreed that it was so great.

I would actually start writing the book itself. The notes could wait. Sure, there was a lot more research to be done, a lot more investigating, a lot more index cards to put in a lot more shoe boxes. But I finally understood the phrase "I thought I might explode!"

I began typing.

Who actually created hell? Some say it was God. Some say it was the devil himself. But if you've ever spent time in New Burg, Nebraska, you would quickly discover that it was neither God nor the devil. Hell was created by a company called the Store.

I pounded away for another half an hour. Maybe longer. I don't remember. I stopped only when I heard Megan open the door and enter.

"Jacob, it's an oven in here. Turn on the air conditioner," she said.

"I will," I said. But I kept typing.

"What are you doing? You're typing like a crazy man," she said.

"I'm doing what I said I'd be doing. I'm working on our project."

"No need to be nasty," she said. "Jacob, you are so sweaty. You look like you've been swimming."

I wanted to say, "Stop talking, goddamn it. I'm thinking." But I ignored her and just kept writing. Finally I stopped. I just stopped. I was a race car that had suddenly run out of gas. I let my head drop to my wet chest. I was breathing heavily. Megan looked concerned.

She ran her hand across my bare back as she sat in the chair next to mine.

"Are you okay?" she said.

"In a way," I answered.

"In a way? What does that mean?"

"I'm not sure," I said.

Megan flipped open her laptop, and I eventually gained enough composure and energy to click over to my e-mail. I looked at the long stack that had accumulated since I first checked it early that morning in San Francisco. My eye immediately went to the e-mail with the subject line written in big red type. URGENT STORE MGMT SF, CA.

I opened it.

Hello, Jacob Brandeis,

We are sorry to inform you that your presence at the Store fulfillment center in New Burg, Nebraska, is no longer required at this moment.

We are sorry for contacting you on such short notice, but circumstances have prevented us from doing so sooner.

In keeping with our ongoing philosophy—No worries—we will be in touch soon with more information regarding your future with the Store.

The e-mail was unsigned.

"Holy shit!" I said softly.

"What's the matter?" Megan asked.

"Holy shit!" I said it again.

"Jacob, what's going on?"

"I think I just lost my job."

CHAPTER 43

FROM THAT moment on everything was different.

Megan and I still awoke early every day. But while she left for her supervisory job at the Store, I went up to our attic office and worked on the book.

I made it my job, and it turned out to be a job that I really loved. I was fueled by my disgust for my former employer, and I was especially fueled by the fact that I had been fired in a painful, careless way. So working on the book was almost like a drug for me. As I slapped away at the keys and constantly rearranged index cards, my heart beat fast and loud. When I made phone calls to informants I hoped could help me—former Store employees, former suppliers, a retired judge in Denver whom the founder, Thomas P. Owens, had briefly clerked for—I was quick and smooth and mildly aggressive. I was, I thought, doing God's work. And other than an occasional break to use the bathroom or nibble on a piece of cheese like a happy rat, I spent all day at my desk.

I was happy at my unpaid freelance job, but I was not happy with my family and my life with them.

All three of them never seemed to tire of reminding me that they had warned me about my behavior. Mind you, they were never mean when the subject came up, but it came up way too frequently.

"How many times did I tell you to calm down and get with the program?" Megan would say.

Then Alex would chime in: "I told you, Dad. I told you more than once that you were losing it."

Megan would circle back around and say something like, "Yeah, even the kids noticed. First we made them change their lives by bringing them out to the middle of nowhere. And when, miraculously, they adjusted—when they even liked it—"

"We *loved* it," Lindsay said, correcting her.

Megan continued: "When they *loved* it, *you* couldn't adjust to it. You had to go mess things up."

We had that conversation, or some variation of that conversation, almost every night and more often on weekends.

If I argued, if I protested, they didn't seem to care. They argued louder and bigger than I could. The refrain they said over and over was, "Why don't you just go back to your office and write your book?"

More than a few times at the beginning of my "retirement" I'd catch the children recording me on video. I might be up in the workroom, deeply involved with the manuscript. I'd stop, feeling the presence of someone who had come into the room, then turn around and see Lindsay or Alex filming me.

"Why? Why?" I'd yell, and their answers would be something between evasive and credible.

"It's for a project on our home life."

"This flat-vid had an upgrade. I'm just trying it out."

"Alex and I are doing this for a video scrapbook. You'll be dead someday, you know."

I would yell, "Just stop it. Please just stop it," and they would roll their eyes with impatience. The children would tell me to "chill," and Megan would tell me pretty much the same thing. "What they're doing is harmless, for God's sake."

Eventually I pretty much grew used to it. I knew, of course, that I should be in charge. I should insist that they stop. I should take the damned flat-vids away. I should argue louder than the three of them. But the simple fact was that all I really cared about was the book.

The more I got pissed off, the more I worked. And because of all that angry energy, the book was moving really fast. It moved even faster when I began the second part, the eyewitness part—based mostly on my phone calls, research, e-mails, letters, and, of course, my own experiences.

Bette and Bud's "transfer." Bette and Bud's barbecue. The no-show founder at the meeting in San Francisco. My treatment at airport security.

My days were filled with energy, and because Megan was usually tired from her supervisory job, I became the book's full-time writer. Megan became the part-time editor.

I usually worked on my manuscript until around 2:00

a.m. Then I checked to make certain that my writing had been saved onto a red flash drive. Once I knew my words were safely recorded I yanked out the flash drive and kept it with me at all times. Quite simply, it never left my sight. That red flash drive was titled simply *Twenty-Twenty*. And someday soon I would be printing its contents—the start of something I was already thinking of as *Store Wars*.

Knowing that this manuscript was safe and growing kept me as calm as I could ever hope to be. I was not angry at the constant carping from my family about "losing it" and "not getting with the program." I was not angry when my children committed my most ordinary moments to video. I was not even angry when Megan quietly opened the bathroom door a crack and made a video of me drying off after a shower.

All I really cared about was the book.

CHAPTER 44

BEEF BRISKET in a sweet-and-sour onion-tomato sauce. Good and lumpy real mashed potatoes. Emerald-green peas mixed with tiny little bits of prosciutto.

It should have been a perfect meal.

"Now, listen," I said. "If you want me to have dinner with you, put every video and recording device away. Agreed?" I said.

"Agreed," Lindsay said.

"I didn't hear you, Alex," I said.

"Agreed," he said. Okay, his voice was sullen—but he said it.

"Megan? What about you?"

"You expect me to take the oath?" she said, only slightly annoyed.

"Yes, ma'am."

"Are you crazy?" she asked.

With a smile I said, "Possibly."

"Oh, my God," Megan said. Then she took a big

breath, let it out, and very softly said, "Agreed." She waited. Then added, just as softly, "And you *are* crazy."

Dinner began.

"No wine for me," I said. "I've got work to do."

Alex asked that Lindsay "please pass the pot roast." Lindsay corrected him and told him it was beef brisket. Megan told them not to start arguing.

As I was taking my first taste of the buttery mashed potatoes, Lindsay said, "How's the book going?"

"Like you care," I said. Why was my voice so venomous, so sarcastic? I often joked with the kids (and Megan) in a funny, teasing way, but all the "how to raise your child" books always advised against anger and sarcasm.

"Jacob," Megan said. "Lindsay was asking a perfectly reasonable question."

But I could not stop.

"Yeah, *you* think it's reasonable. But I know it's *not* reasonable."

Alex looked down at his dinner plate. Lindsay took a big gulp from her water glass.

"My book. My book. My book." I was shaking my head. What was the matter with me?

"Maybe you're spending too much time working on your book, your book, your book," Alex said.

I stared at him with open, angry eyes.

"We've told you. The three of us. Give up on the book."

Then Lindsay spoke loudly, with volume and irritation in her voice: *"You just don't understand!"*

In a scary, soft tone, I said, "Oh...but that's where you're all wrong...I absolutely do understand.

"I understand what a magnificently evil, powerful machine the subject of my book..."

"*Our* book," Megan said, correcting me.

Now I was really pissed.

"No, Megan. It's *my* book. You and *your* children have done nothing but try to get me to stop. Well, I've got news for you. I will not stop. I know what a powerful machine the Store is. No one knows as much as I do. No one has looked at it so closely."

I stood up, and in my mind I was as inspiring as King Arthur addressing the Round Table, as wise as Christ at the Last Supper.

And for the first time I realized that Megan and the kids might be right: I was crazy.

"Yes. They'll come for me. Like soldiers, like Nazis, in the middle of the night. They'll take me, and they'll take my book."

There was no structure to my thoughts. As the ideas came to my head I vomited the words out into the air.

"They know what I'm up to. They know everything. The Store is more powerful than anyone or anything. Nobody can escape it—especially a little nobody like me. The surveillance cameras. The recording devices. The spies at work. The spies in the San Francisco hotels. The drones. The neighbors who are not really neighbors. The friends who are not really friends. The family who..." I had to stop there.

Alex's eyes had not moved from his downward stare at his plate. Lindsay's hand was shaking as it held her water glass. Megan's eyes were wet.

"I am *not* prepared for their arrival. Nobody can be. But I will be strong about it all. The exposé will go on. They can steal my book. They can burn my book. But the truth will come out.

"You three are wrong. You preach at me to stop. You plead with me to stop. But you three are totally wrong. Totally.

"What you don't understand is this: *I do understand!*"

CHAPTER 45

"GET THE hell off my property," I screamed.

"Brandeis, we are here to enforce a town and state request," said one of the two men banging their fists on our front door.

"I said get the hell off my property."

It was three o'clock on a Saturday afternoon. Cold and cloudy, and the weather was not made pleasanter by the fact that my family and I were barely speaking to one another.

"Brandeis, let us in or we'll have to use force," said the same guy.

Both men wore cheap-looking gray suits. One guy was tall and white and blond. The other guy was tall and black and bald. Both of them were annoyingly handsome. Both of them were alarmingly large. I figured that neither of them was from New Burg, because neither of them was smiling.

"Let them in, Jacob," Megan said. "Why are you always fighting, always causing problems?"

I took a deep breath and began unlocking the door.

The second I had completed the job, precisely when the door was unlocked, the blond guy put his hand through the open space and pushed me violently into the hallway. I fell to the floor. The bald guy was carrying a sledgehammer, which he used to smash the knob from the door. One quick and powerful movement. That door would be staying unlocked.

"What's this all—" I started to speak but was immediately interrupted by the bald-headed guy.

"Jacob Brandeis, sir?" he said, exactly as I imagined an army sergeant leading basic training would say it. I was pulling myself up off the floor.

"I'm asking you what this—" I tried again. The blond guy spoke next.

"Answer, sir. Are you Jacob Brandeis?" He was even more hostile.

"Look—" I tried yet again.

"Jacob Brandeis? Answer me, sir. Answer me *now!*"

Megan decided to answer for me.

"Yes. He's Jacob Brandeis." Her voice was cold, precise.

The bald guy said, "Your computer, Brandeis."

"No," I said.

"Give us your computer, Brandeis."

"Maybe you didn't hear me," I said.

The blond guy now: "Your computer, Brandeis."

Then, like a little kid, I said, "You can't make me." I was nervous, and, of course, I felt like a sniveling six-year-old in front of my family.

"It's in his attic workroom," Lindsay said. Like her mother's, my daughter's voice was quiet but stern.

"You *cannot* come into my house like this and ask for me to give you *my* things."

"Yes, they can, Jacob," Megan said.

At that moment the blond guy grabbed hold of my upper arms with his hands and pulled me from the stairway landing. He flung me to the hall floor. The bald guy ran up the stairs, hurdling every three steps. The other guy was right behind him. I stood up and was about to follow them.

Megan yelled, "Stop your dad!"

To my astonishment, Alex made a lame attempt to push me back down. I ran up the stairs and arrived in the attic at the same moment one of the intruders was folding the power cord around my closed laptop. The other guy was making uneven stacks of every piece of paper—scraps, printouts, index cards—on my desk. I briefly noticed that neither of the men had taken Megan's computer.

CHAPTER 46

"DO YOU have any other electronic equipment, Brandeis?" the bald guy said. The skin on his head glistened with sweat.

I just looked at him.

"Do you?" he repeated.

"You know as well as I do what I have," I said.

"Check," the guy said. He and his colleague each took plastic garbage bags from their briefcases and emptied the contents of the wastebaskets into them. They also swept the three unsorted, uneven stacks of papers from my desk into their bags. Then they pulled some loose planks from the steep incline under the roof. All they found was asbestos padding. Of course, I hoped they'd die from being so close to the toxic material.

The bald guy and the blond guy then saw an unlocked trunk. They flipped open the top. Nothing but old CDs (Ludacris, anyone?), old college books (*Middlemarch*, anyone?), and old children's drawings ("My Dad mak god raveoli"). They felt the inner sides of the trunk for secret panels. They seemed very pissed off that they found nothing incriminating. For me it was a small pleasure, but it was a pleasure nonetheless.

Megan and Alex and Lindsay appeared at the doorway. Megan shook her head gently. The children? I don't know. I'm not sure. Were they smug? Were they sad? Did they find me pathetic? Foolish? I couldn't tell, and I regret to say that I was on the verge of not giving a shit.

"Brandeis, we've finished our search-and-gather," said the blond guy.

"Search-and-gather?" I said. "That's what you call it? It's a basic violation of every American privacy law. But frankly, I don't give a shit. It's exactly what I was expecting."

I surveyed the strangely uncluttered room. The men stood next to their respective black garbage bags. The bald-headed guy read aloud from a large card:

"Jacob Brandeis, the town and city of New Burg, in the state of Nebraska, have rightfully collected, with approval from the offices of the Nebraska Department of Justice, item or items that are considered of governmental consequence to the people of the state. This material may or may not be returned to you upon completion of examination."

There was a pause. Then, continuing to read, the bald-headed guy said:

"Do you understand the statement I have just read to you?"

"Sure," I said. "And you can all burn in hell."

CHAPTER 47

IT WAS precisely 5:00 a.m. I carefully got out of bed.

Megan seemed to be sleeping soundly, making tiny sharp nasal sounds somewhere between snoring and loud breathing. I quietly opened the bedroom door and stepped out, closing it behind me. Then I briefly held my ear to the door of Alex's room. Heavy snoring. Then I listened at the door to Lindsay's room. I wasn't absolutely certain that she wasn't awake, but no light drifted into the hallway from under her bedroom door. I was pretty sure that my three housemates were asleep.

I walked up the stairway to my barren workroom. Then I removed the red flash drive from my jeans pocket. I snapped the little piece into Megan's laptop and typed:

TWENTY-TWENTY
The True Story of the Store
by
Jacob Brandeis

I pressed Save, then ejected the red flash drive and returned it to my jeans pocket.

I had stashed my backpack behind two stacks of old *BusinessWeek* magazines. The backpack itself was filled with a change of clothing, a toothbrush, toothpaste, a yellow legal pad, two pens, a bottle of Lipitor, a fifth of Jack Daniel's, and my iPad, newly loaded with a bunch of classic novels and the first two seasons of *House of Cards*.

I was ready to go.

I closed the door to my workroom and headed down the attic stairs. As I passed by a closed bedroom door I heard a stage whisper: "Daddy, where are you going?"

It was Lindsay.

"I'll be back in a little bit. Don't worry," I said.

The breathy, rasping whisper followed me downstairs: "You really are crazy," she said.

Only I could hear my response.

"So I've heard."

CHAPTER 48

I TOSSED my backpack and a six-pack of Fresca on the passenger seat. With all the surveillance cameras hanging from trees and stoplights, I couldn't race away, but let's just say that I challenged the speed limit.

Where was I headed? The only destination I had in mind was "anyplace that isn't this place." Away from my absurd family and town. I was, deep down inside, also hoping to escape from myself—from my overwhelming fear and paranoia.

I quickly arrived at Interstate 80, the highway that runs from California to New Jersey. I had no idea whether to head west or east. Then I thought: *Hey, what about the ski instructor who taught the kids two years ago, when we were on vacation in Vail?* Amy and I had become very friendly; Megan thought we had become way too friendly, which, just to let you know, was absolutely untrue. I could call her. She'd remember me. Then my brain returned, and I realized she would have no memory of who I was.

Bette and Bud were obviously out, and with the

pathetic realization that I had no close friends west of the Mississippi, I headed east on I-80. At least I had a former college friend in some Chicago suburb, and I was pretty sure that my cousin the kidney specialist lived in Saint Louis.

The highway was surprisingly busy for just after 5:00 a.m. My guesses: trucks hauling pigs and cows to slaughterhouses; tankards filled with corn oil, a Nebraska specialty; high-striving yuppies off to their cubicles at the Store.

The farther I drove, the better I felt. The better I felt, the more certain I was that my book, *Twenty-Twenty*, was marked for success. *The timing is absolutely perfect,* I thought, slamming both fists on the steering wheel as I reached the outskirts of Lincoln.

By seven o'clock that morning I was about to cross the state border into Iowa. It was then that I had what could modestly be called a brainstorm: I would call Anne Gutman, my editor at Writers Place. Sure, she had screwed me over a little by rejecting my and Megan's music book, but I knew Anne had faith in me. And I knew she would see how hot my manuscript was.

Yes. *Twenty-Twenty*. The phrase "marked for success" kept running through my mind. "Marked for success," like George Orwell's *1984*. His exposé of a cultural nightmare was off by thirty-six years.

Twenty-Twenty would be right on target.

CHAPTER 49

ONCE ANNE Gutman got over the initial shock of hearing my voice on the phone, she said something I hadn't heard in a long time.

"You're in luck." Then she added, "I have a friend who lives east of Des Moines in a sweet little town called Goosen Valley. Her name is Maggie Pine, and five years ago she did a magnificent coffee-table book for me on Mennonite quilts."

Thirty minutes later I was sitting and eating warm blueberry muffins in a kitchen in Goosen Valley, Iowa. The kitchen had an oak Hoosier cabinet and a collection of nineteenth-century mixing bowls, and Maggie Pine had a sweet face that would prompt a normal human being to trust her. I guess I was no longer a normal human being, because the charming kitchen seemed cold, and Maggie's sweet face felt unfriendly...at least to me.

While Maggie went upstairs to wash her face and "run a brush through my mop," I walked around the backyard herb garden. The basil was sparse and dying. The rosemary plants were still standing tall. And a little plant sign that said BORAGE (I had never heard of it) stood beneath a giant ugly clump of weedy-looking green leaves.

On the walk to her tiny newspaper office at the *Goosen Register* (Margaret Pine, editor and only full-time reporter), my new friend and hostess told me how "wonderfully helpful" Anne Gutman had been to her when she was "assembling and writing my quilt tome."

"She had me to New York City two times, and she put me up in a hotel on Fifth Avenue with a view of Central Park, hardly a place to think about Mennonite quilts, but I managed."

As we walked through the small downtown, I was amazed at how much it resembled New Burg. But this town was real, and by "real" I mean "really real." The ice cream parlor had a hand-lettered sign above the door that said FOUR GREAT FLAVORS. The library exterior was a harsh mixture of old brick and new aluminum siding. Even the bookstore, called Good Books and Good Things, had a window that held not only books but also other items for sale: china teapots made to resemble cats, school supplies, jars of orange marmalade. New Burg wanted to be just like Goosen Valley; it just couldn't do it.

"Is there enough news in this town to fill a weekly newspaper?" I asked Maggie as we sat in her storefront office and she zipped quickly through her e-mail.

"Well, we do the usual. One of the local teachers, he does the high school sports news. Everyone cares about that. Then I have a part-time woman who does the social news, such as it is. That's birthday parties and anniversary parties and church news. But . . . now, don't you go thinking we're just a bunch of farmers. We have a monthly book club and read important books, and I don't mean *Fifty Shades of Grey*. A retired doctor wrote a very thoughtful piece on eldercare and dementia. And when I did an editorial endorsing same-sex marriage, only two e-mails to the editor criticized me. Thirty-four others cheered me on."

I threw my hands up in the air.

"You got me. Clearly Goosen Valley is the Paris of the Midwest. And I don't mean that sarcastically. I wish New Burg had been more like this town," I said.

"Look," Maggie said. "Anne gave me a brief synopsis of your problems, at least as she understands them after a short phone conversation. All I can say is that I hope you make peace with yourself. You can stay at my place until you're ready to move on, Jacob. And with any luck . . ."

Suddenly from outside I heard a very big thud. It was mixed with the sound of a buzzing motor. My head snapped toward the storefront window.

"Not to worry," Maggie said. "It's just a drone delivery."

CHAPTER 50

THAT NIGHT Maggie Pine fed me honey-glazed roasted chicken, lump-free mashed turnips, and, of course, corn on the cob made perfect with lots of butter and salt.

Maggie was a very pretty red-haired woman, but this pretty woman and this great-tasting meal did not make me long for Maggie. It made me long for the old days in New York with Megan and Alex and Lindsay around the table. I really wanted to phone my family, but I stopped myself every time the idea tempted me. I knew it would be a stupid thing, a really stupid thing, to contact them. Tomorrow I'd be back on the road again. Maybe I'd feel different. Maybe then I'd call, or the next day...or the next...or...

The guest bedroom in Maggie's house was straight out of a bed-and-breakfast catalog: a canopy bed with a whole bunch of decorative pillows. The room was also a kind of Mennonite quilt museum—one quilt on the bed, two folded at the foot of the bed, and five others on an old steamer trunk under the window.

I tried reading one of the books I'd grabbed from Maggie's shelf, *The Good Earth*. It only made me wonder how they figured that book deserved the Pulitzer Prize back then.

I tossed. Then I turned. Then I tossed some more. I remembered what my mother used to say: "When you can't sleep, it means you've got a guilty conscience." I got up and out of bed.

When I walked to the window I could see the dark images of "downtown" Goosen Valley, a model of Americana, complete with steeple and water tower. Closer to my window were the branches of a tree that Maggie had identified as an ancient black walnut. The sun was just rising, darkness outside beginning to build to light. Two tiny stars, still hanging on in the morning light, sparkled through the branches of the black walnut tree.

Everything was peaceful for a moment. Even me.

CHAPTER 51

MAYBE I had slept a little bit. Maybe for a few minutes? A half hour? Maybe I had just fallen asleep sitting on the window ledge? Maybe... oh, what the hell difference did it make? Here I was on a chair near the window in Maggie Pine's guest bedroom. And it was suddenly morning. And I was sort of awake. And I could really use a shower to get totally awake.

As I walked to the little bathroom attached to the bedroom I noticed a small framed antique sampler hanging on the wall. It said that it was created by a girl named Marie D in the year 1822. It was a line from the Bible:

Watch therefore, for ye know neither the day nor the hour wherein the Son of man cometh.

I sure couldn't argue with that.

The bathroom had no shower, only a tub. Bathing in a tub never made sense to me. I'm not a guy who likes soaking in his own dirty water. So I did my best to wash away the previous day's dirt and sweat by kneeling in front of the bathtub faucet. I let the water run, and I bent my head forward to wash my hair. Then I alternately soaped myself up and splashed myself off to get rid of the soap.

On the small table near the tub were the perfect props for such a quaint little bathroom: dried flowers in a Mason jar, an engraved antique silver hand mirror, and a matching silver comb. Also on the table was a tin of Yardley talcum powder—lily of the valley.

I dried myself with a big white towel, then I made a decision that was, for me, a daring one. I doused myself with a lot of the floral-scented powder.

Because I'd left the bathroom door open, I had no trouble hearing the knock on the bedroom door. Then the door squeaked open.

"Jacob," I heard. "Jacob. It's just me, Maggie."

"Hold on," I yelled back. "I just took a shower... er...not a shower...I just took a bath. What's up?"

I asked this question with a slight nervousness in my voice, all the while wrapping the towel around me and securing it as firmly as I could.

Before I went back into the bedroom, I glanced at myself in the old mirror over the sink. I tell you—not with phony modesty—I was not a particularly handsome sight: chest hair made grayish white with talcum powder, along with my ridiculously skinny arms and equally skinny legs.

"Almost caught me," I said to Maggie.

"I'm sorry. I should have waited for you to answer the door."

"It's okay. We're friends," I said, and I'm sure I had one of those grins that's usually called sheepish or stupid or both.

"I brought some coffee and a little flask of orange juice." As she spoke she gestured toward the table next to the narrow bed. Sure enough, there was a wooden tray with a delicate little cup, steam rising out of it, and a small cut-glass container of orange juice.

"You look tired, Jacob," Maggie said.

"Yeah, I'm not even sure that I fell asleep. When that happens you really know you had a bad night."

At the foot of the bed was an undershirt. I slipped it over my head, but I then suddenly worried that by moving my arms into the armholes I'd be pulling in my waist and end up losing my towel.

"Here," Maggie said. "Let me help."

She walked toward me.

"Hey, you used the lily of the valley stuff," she said. "I like that so much. It reminds me of my grandmother."

"Great. I very often remind girls of their grandmothers."

She laughed, and she stretched the undershirt over my shoulders. All the while I held on to the towel knot.

Maggie was about to pull the undershirt down over me when she brushed her hand hard against my chest. A fairly small puff of white powder erupted.

She put her hand back on my chest. Then she spoke.

"So whaddya think?" she said.

For a few moments I said nothing. And for those same moments she did nothing.

Finally it was Maggie who spoke.

"I guess not," she said.

"Well . . ." I paused. Then I added, "I guess not."

She walked to the bedroom door and told me to drink my coffee and take my time. She'd be downstairs. She'd make some toast. Or did I want something else? She could make some corn muffins. No; toast was fine. Actually I never eat breakfast. Cereal, maybe. She had some old Rice Krispies. No. No, thank you . . . then she suddenly walked out of the room and closed the door behind her.

I don't think I breathed a sigh of relief, but I was relieved. I was also sad.

I must have looked ridiculous: my undershirt half on, my towel coming undone. I brushed as much of her grandma-smelling powder off me as I could.

It was my intention to sip my coffee, drink my orange juice, and take my time getting dressed.

But that was not going to happen.

CHAPTER 52

"JACOB! GET down here! Now!"

It took me a moment to recognize Maggie's voice.

Suddenly I heard sirens. Bright light poured through the bedroom window.

"Jacob! Please! Hurry!"

I left my peaceful view of a Goosen Valley morning. Wearing only my white undershirt and white boxers, I ran from the bedroom and shot down the stairs two at a time.

In the small front hallway was Maggie Pine with a crowd of people, at least a dozen of them, two or three of them spilling out through the open front door. It took me only a few seconds to realize that this was neither a fire response nor police activity. These were people I actually knew: Megan, Alex, Lindsay. Surrounding my family were Sam and Bette and Bud. Holy shit. There was the neighborhood leader, Marie DiManno.

The faces that were familiar to me but also nameless were the young man and woman who had "interviewed" us in San Francisco as well as the two thuglike men who had appropriated my laptop and private papers only a couple of nights ago in New Burg.

"What in hell is going on?" I said—quietly, full of confusion, amazement.

"We're all here to help," said Maggie.

Oh, my God. So Maggie was in on it, too.

"What the hell is this?" I said. My eyes and head whirled from one face to another. The faces were sad-looking, serious.

"Help with what?" I was yelling now.

Lindsay stepped forward and took my hand in hers. She spoke the way you might address a three-year-old who's dropped his ice cream cone.

"This is an intervention, Daddy."

I snapped my hand back from her grip. "This is bull-shit!" I said.

My anger was apparently a signal for the two thugs—the bald guy and the blond guy—to step forward and prepare to hold me back. As they moved, I could see through the door. A news truck. A sound truck. Four men and two women. Two of them wore headphones, two of them held boom mikes.

This intervention was being filmed.

The interview woman stepped forward and stood beside Lindsay.

Her voice was dramatically soft and sweet. "Let's try to stay calm. Maybe we can go somewhere to talk quietly. Is that possible, Ms. Pine?"

"Of course. Let's move into the dining room. I fixed it so there'd be room for everyone."

As the crowd moved, joined by some of the film crew, I was almost shoved bodily past the staircase and into the dining room.

Maggie had pushed her old pine dining table against the wall and arranged the chairs—the regular dining chairs and a bunch of folding chairs—in a semicircle.

"I'm in my goddamn underwear," I shouted.

Megan touched my shoulder and tried to nudge me gently into the center chair. This was the first time my wife had spoken.

"Sweetie, don't be so formal. It doesn't matter what you're wearing."

"Of course it matters," I said angrily. "It only doesn't matter if someone is crazy...if someone is a goddamn mental patient. All of you, get the hell out of here."

No one reacted. No one lost his or her temper.

So that was it? They thought I was crazy, and they were going to treat me as a crazy person?

Only for a moment did I think they might be right. I thought it as I looked down at my bare legs, at the filthy soles of my naked feet, at the glazed look on my children's faces. Bette was silently mouthing words. A prayer, maybe? The two interviewers were taking notes on their handheld devices. The thugs were seated on either side of me. Just in case.

But the thought of madness evaporated as fast as it had appeared. I was angry. I was foolish, perhaps. But I was certainly not crazy. And I suddenly knew more than ever that the manuscript had to get to Anne Gutman. And I knew just how to do that.

CHAPTER 53

"WE ARE all worried—very, very worried about you, Jacob."

Bud was talking.

"You know it, Dad," Alex said. He crossed in front of his mother and sister, stood in front of me, and, facing me, placed his hands on my shoulders. This was definitely not Alex's style. Who the hell was this kid?

Meanwhile the sound guy held the boom over whoever might be talking. Three cameramen moved softly around the room, one of them filming whoever was speaking, another filming "reaction shots," the third concentrating entirely on me.

Bette, Lindsay, and the woman interviewer from San Francisco all contributed to the intervention. They carried the theme of caring and understanding and the need for help to a nauseating level. Literally, my stomach rumbled. My chest ached with anger. Perhaps the most over-the-top piece of madness came from Lindsay.

After she carried on tearfully about my inability to focus on my family, my wife, and my children—"the people who are here to bring you joy"—she looked squarely into my eyes and said, "I want my father back."

I wanted to scream at my daughter, "You make me sick." Instead I stood up and spoke in a calm, normal tone: "Please. Why don't you all just leave me alone?" Then I yelled at the top of my lungs: "Please!"

At that the two thugs standing behind me moved closer, just in case I needed to be subdued.

My crazy brain was suddenly elsewhere: I needed to find a way to escape. I had to find a way. What I considered a compelling and important book a few days ago I now thought of as something way beyond a masterpiece, a book that would conquer evil and deliver freedom before it was too late. Was I just another crazy man, or was I carrying what was essentially the fifth Gospel?

I wasn't sure. But I had to keep fighting.

The interview guy from San Francisco stood up and moved smack-dab in front of me. He spoke slowly and deliberately and kept inserting an especially maddening phrase into his speech: "Do you understand me, Jacob?"

I shook with anger. My eyes filled with tears. My undershirt was drenched with sweat.

"We are here to help you. Do you understand me, Jacob? We are going to bring you back to New Burg and enter you into a treatment and behavior renewal clinic, where you will relearn the concepts of joyful living. Do you understand me, Jacob? We all believe—your family, your friends, specialists from the psychotherapy group at the Store—that within four or five weeks you will be better and stronger and happier. Do you understand me, Jacob?"

As he spoke, the intervention group began surrounding me. Despite their soft words and pitiful faces, they were scaring me. I felt strangely like the victim of a lynch mob.

"We'll be with you, Daddy," Lindsay said.

"I love you, sweetie," Megan said.

"I warned you about that book, Dad," Alex said.

The two thugs were on either side of my chair now.

Bud spoke in almost a whisper.

"It'll be the best thing for you, Jake. Don't be mad. Don't be angry."

The tears dribbled out of my eyes. I could taste the saltiness sneaking into my mouth. I could see my naked knees shaking.

I knew it was because of my sheer fury at their brazen intervention.

They thought they had convinced me of the wisdom of their mission.

My tears came harder now. I stood up. The thugs put their hands firmly around my elbows and wrists.

"Stop it! Please stop it!" I yelled.

I sat down, and I quietly said what I had to say.

"I understand. I do. I thank you all. I'll do what you want me to do."

CHAPTER 54

IT WORKED.

Man, I thought. *If I'm still alive next year when they give out the Oscars they've got to give one to me.* Bette and Bud and Marie dripped tears like three waterfalls. My kids and my wife hugged me and thanked me. The woman from the San Francisco interview called me a good man. The bald-headed thug called me a wise man. Maggie Pine said she hoped I'd be a forgiving man.

"I was brought into this intervention at the very end," she added.

"Does our friend Anne know about all this?" I asked.

"Oh, no. Only this small intervention group knows about it," she said. Maggie shared a knowing smile with Megan, two bitches in cahoots. The blond thug standing beside me joined in the sickening smile.

Maggie walked off toward the kitchen. The blond guy said he needed to speak with me. This bastard who had invaded my home and stolen my things was now talking like the sweetest guy on earth.

Megan and the kids paid very close attention as he spoke.

"So here's the plan, Jake."

Jake?

"One of our people will drive your car back to New Burg. Now, there are a few other cars that we brought along. One will take your family to their house. So you and I and Cue Ball..."

I stopped paying attention right there. The bald guy was called Cue Ball? Does a bald guy like being called Cue Ball? And aren't cue balls usually white? This guy was black. And he must have a real name, a given name...

"Mr. Brandeis, are you listening?" the blond guy asked.

Mr. Brandeis. No more Jake. No more last name only, as it was when he stole my laptop, wrecked my office, set me off on this madness.

"Yes, of course," I said.

"As I said, you and I and Cue Ball will drive back to New Burg in our own car. It will have a driver and a driving assistant..."

I spoke: "You mean a driver and a guard."

"No. I mean a driver and a driving assistant, should anything happen to the driver."

Okay, Jacob, go back to acting like the cooperative patient they want. Just keep it up. Play nice. And, most important, figure out how to escape.

"We should get going," the blond guy said. "Do you have anything up in your room that you absolutely need?"

"*Absolutely need?* Maybe you noticed that I'm standing here in my underwear."

"Okay, let's go up and put your clothes on."

"What are you gonna do? Zip my fly?"

That wise-guy line put me back on his shit list.

"Let's go," he said.

"You need coffee," Maggie Pine yelled. She was carrying a large tray that held a big pot of coffee and a lot of paper cups. We walked a few feet to the dining-room table.

As she handed the blond guy a cup, she said, "Cream and sugar?"

"Just black," he said.

"Me, too," I said. "We're going up to get my things. Then we're leaving."

"I thought so," Maggie said.

In my best sarcastic tone of voice I said, "By the way, thanks for everything."

"Sure," she said. "Just be sure to check the bathroom cabinet. Make certain you didn't forget anything."

"I will," I said.

CHAPTER 55

I SLIPPED into my jeans. I slipped into my army-green T-shirt. I slipped into my old red-and-white Nikes.

The blond guy gave the inside of my backpack a thorough search. The most illicit thing he could find was my bottle of bourbon.

I glanced out the window. It was full morning now, and I realized that what I had earlier thought were stars twinkling through the branches of the walnut tree were—*Holy shit! Of course!*—surveillance cameras.

"I need to slap some water on my face, and I need to pee," I said.

"Yeah, sure," he said. I guess we were friends again. "Only leave the door open."

I walked into the bathroom, left the door ajar by a foot or so, turned on the faucet to a quick drip. I hoped it sounded like a guy urinating.

When I opened the linen closet in the bathroom, I glanced from top to bottom—Martha Stewart towels, Crabtree & Evelyn soap, Caswell-Massey body lotion.

Sort of what I expected. What I didn't expect was a two-foot-tall cabinet below the lowest shelf. When I pulled open the drawer, it turned out to be a false wooden front. It fell to the floor.

From the bedroom: "That's the longest piss I've ever heard. What'd ya do, have a few Buds before bedtime?"

I don't know if he said anything more. By that time I had seen the window at the rear of the closet. Under the sill was an attached rope ladder as well as a small envelope. The envelope had pencil writing on the front: GOOD LUCK. MAGGIE. Inside the envelope were my car keys.

I unrolled the rope ladder out the window and down the side of the house.

It took me around thirty seconds to make it to the ground. It took another thirty seconds to get to Maggie's garden. I knelt down and dug up my little red flash drive. It was wrapped in aluminum foil and was near the huge borage plant. Exactly where I had buried it yesterday morning.

I ran to my car. A quarter of a tank of gas. I took off. No headlights on. No seat belt fastened.

As I drove away from the house all I could say, over and over again, was "God bless Maggie Pine."

CHAPTER 56

FEAR. CHAOS. And hell. Not necessarily in that order.

Okay, I made it out of the insane intervention, but I was in a huge pile of trouble. I got an idea of how huge the minute I drove out of Maggie Pine's mud-and-cobblestone driveway. The auto-info—the car speaker that came on automatically when the Store had an announcement that they wanted broadcast immediately—blasted out at me:

"A person of suspicious and possibly harmful nature is at large. His last known location was the Nebraska-Iowa border. His name is Jacob Brandeis. Male, midforties, white. He is wearing red-and-white shoes. Photos and more details of subject are available on all electronic devices, electronic billboards, and electronic posters. If you see Jacob Brandeis or anyone resembling Jacob Brandeis, text STORE 134."

This announcement, which would be repeated every five minutes, was replaced by a Jay Z song played backwards.

If I had any doubt that I was a crazy man on a crazy flight, less than two miles away from Maggie Pine's house was a large electronic poster, a composite of a white male in his forties. He didn't look harmful, but he sure as hell looked exactly like me—right down to his scruffy T-shirt and two-day growth of beard.

The first thing I realized was that if I had even a slight chance of succeeding in this escape I had to ditch the car. By now, I was a major expert on how the Store operated, and I knew that the Store would be quickly broadcasting more information: GPS coordinates, car description, license-plate number, locations of former friends (a few) and current friends (not many). The Store would be relentless. I was a weak little rabbit being chased by the psycho equivalent of the United States Marines.

What the hell could I do? Run through the Iowa cornfield like some asshole in a bad B movie?

It was a small miracle that my sweaty, dirty hands could hold on to the steering wheel.

Suddenly Jay Z was interrupted by a repeat of the previous announcement. They were going to find Jacob Brandeis. A guy who wrote a book was as big a threat as a kidnapper or a terrorist.

When the auto-info ended, no other sound returned. The digital speedometer and engine gauges went dead. The car kept moving, but the brakes were feeling shaky. Not failing completely, but failing. The Store had, remotely, disconnected anything that could be disconnected.

Amazingly, after what I estimated to be around five miles of driving, I still had not seen another car—one truck and two tractors, but no car. Of course I assumed that this lack of traffic was part of the plot to capture me, and it seemed like just the sort of creepy, scary method the Store would use. I also knew that it was only a matter of time before the drones would be sailing over me.

I saw four more electronic posters and two electronic billboards with new and enhanced photos of me. One even had a separate rendering of my dirty red-and-white sneakers.

I kept driving, and I kept thinking that some great mother of an idea would hit me. But the only thing that hit me were those posters and those now incessant auto-info broadcasts.

This was truly hell on wheels.

Shit, man. I was a goddamn fugitive.

CHAPTER 57

YOU HAVEN'T tasted the putrid combination of fear and depression until you've stood in the Greyhound bus station in Carolton, Iowa. A tattered billboard half a mile earlier had said BUS STATION. GO GREYHOUND. And it was the first sign of hope that I had encountered since I had escaped the "intervention" at Maggie Pine's house.

I left my car in the rear of an abandoned gas station on the outskirts of town, although it was hard to tell where the town ended and the outskirts began. Then, with my head down, I shuffled toward the bus station. It was a small gray wooden building that looked more like a small saloon in an old western.

Inside, the station was almost empty except for a good-looking teenage boy, blond, skinny, rimless glasses. He sat behind the small counter. The kid was reading on an iPad, and I'm sure he hadn't noticed me enter.

On one of the two wooden benches was a pudgy middle-aged woman knitting. I assumed she was waiting for a bus, but she didn't have a suitcase or even a pocket-book. She was just sitting and knitting.

On the other bench sat a man around seventy years old. All I need to tell you about him is that he smelled distinctly like a dirty men's room.

I got the young guy's attention, and he very politely asked, "Where you going, sir?"

"Well, when's the next bus coming by?"

"It should be here in an hour," he said. "But that depends on if the driver stopped in Walkersville for some liquid refreshment."

"Where's the bus headed after here?"

"Next stop is Garrettville, then Independence, then it goes straight to Springfield, Illinois," the man said.

"That's where the Simpsons live," I said.

He smiled. "You're not the first person to make that joke."

"I guess I'm not. It's just—"

Then the old stinky guy spoke. He didn't yell, but his voice was strong enough for the young man and me to easily hear him.

"I think that's him," the old man said to nobody in particular.

The woman who was knitting ignored him completely. A woman who's knitting is not usually interested in talking to a bum who smells of piss.

"That guy is the guy," the old man said. He was looking directly at us. He was also clearly drunk.

"Mister," the old guy said. "Aren't you the guy...you know...the guy?"

The woman finally spoke. "Hush up," she said. "You old souse."

The old man looked at the slow-moving ceiling fan. Then he seemed to lose interest. But I was extremely interested.

"Before I buy my ticket to Springfield, is there someplace I can get a soda and a sandwich around here?" I asked.

"A soda?"

"You know—a pop, a Coke."

"Yeah. Four doors to the left is Cappy's. It's not bad if they have the pork shoulder today."

"I'll be back in five minutes," I said. As I headed to the door, the lady who was knitting looked at me carefully. The old guy was snoring.

I walked as fast as I could toward my car. I passed Cappy's. (I'd live with my hunger and thirst.) I passed a small True Value hardware store and an empty barbershop. In ten minutes I was back at the abandoned gas station.

There was only one problem. My car was gone.

I looked to my right and to my left six or seven times, as if I might just have misplaced the damn car. Then I realized I couldn't do anything but use my feet. I could either walk or I could give myself up. I touched the flash drive, safe in my pocket, and I started walking.

That little plastic technobullet in my pocket worked like a good luck charm. I wasn't walking more than five minutes when a semi pulled up right alongside me and stopped.

CHAPTER 58

"TEN DOLLARS. Jump in if you got it. Jump back if you ain't."

This proposal was offered by a greasy-looking teenager who could have been the evil twin of the Greyhound ticket seller in Carolton. His bare feet just made it to the pedals of the truck. His hair was slicked back, and the black onyx (I'm guessing it was onyx) piercing on the side of his nose was almost as big as the nose itself. He was smoking weed.

I guess I didn't respond to his offer fast enough to suit him.

"You in or you out, man?" he asked.

I did what I had to do: I hopped in and handed him two fives.

"And you're going where?" I asked.

"More important, where are you going?" he said.

"Ultimately I need to be in New York."

"Well, you are extremely out of luck, 'cause this baby stops in Naperville, Illinois."

"Closer to New York than I am right now," I said. I was determined to sound like a casual wise guy instead of the scared, hungry, nervous, filthy mess that I actually was.

I looked at the clock on the dashboard.

"Holy shit," I said. "It's noon already."

"It's eleven o'clock," he said. "I always keep the clock an hour ahead of time. It gives me something to look forward to."

I didn't quite understand that sentence. And I wasn't really all that happy riding with a stoned driver who could pass for a thirteen-year-old.

We drove in silence for a few minutes.

"You got a name?" the driver said.

"Yeah. I'm George," I said.

George? Where the hell did that come from?

"Was you ever president of the country, George?" he asked, and then he laughed loudly, as if he had just told an incredibly funny joke.

"And your name?" I asked.

"Kenny. And no one named Kenny was ever president." He laughed at this joke even more loudly.

Then he said, "I think we both could use some food. Open the glove compartment."

I did. It was filled with five packages of Hostess cupcakes.

"Take as many as you want. Dinner is covered in the admission price. Gimme a pack. I want to hold off the munchies best I can."

As I was unwrapping the cellophane from the cupcakes the dashboard speaker blasted out a short siren and shot out the announcement about the *possibly dangerous* guy who was on the loose. The news was that the *middle-aged white guy, Jacob Brandeis by name,* was reported *possibly* in the areas of Iowa, Illinois, or Missouri. He had *not* been spotted in screenings at airports or hotels, and—in an unusual burst of Store honesty—*the suspect's tracking location is uncertain.*

I kept my eye on the young driver. Even when the announcer mentioned those red-and-white shoes the kid didn't cast a glance at my feet. He seemed totally occupied licking crumbs and fake whipped cream from his lips.

"These cupcakes are good," I said.

He ignored me. He was way too busy flashing his brights at the "dumbass mother" car in front of us.

I slept.

CHAPTER 59

IT WAS dark night when I woke up.

The truck was parked somewhere on the side of the highway. I assumed it was still I-80. But I couldn't be sure, and I had no immediate way of finding out. The driver was not there.

I got out of the truck and left the door open so I could have a little light. I walked a few feet into the woods and urinated. As soon as I zipped up I heard my traveling companion's voice.

"Hey, we both had the same idea," he said. He was walking toward me from a spot deeper in the woods, and I thought that perhaps the friendliness in his voice came from the new big fat joint he was smoking. We both walked the short distance back to the truck.

He handed me a Thermos. "You thirsty?" he asked.

I was thirsty as hell, but I suddenly had a ridiculous, nauseating feeling: I didn't want to drink from a container where this punk's lips had been. The punk must have been a mind reader.

"Don't worry, man. I look like a scuz, but I don't have any disease."

I took a gulp and almost immediately choked.

"What the hell is that?" I asked.

"Tequila, OJ, and Amaretto. Wicked good."

"Plain wicked. You got anything else?"

"Whaddya think this is for ten bucks a night? The goddamn Hilton?"

He laughed, but I didn't think he was happy. We climbed back into the truck.

"Where are we?" I said as he drove us back on the highway.

He didn't answer, but he tossed me a cheap stand-alone GPS unit.

"See for yourself," he said. (I think he was still pissed that I didn't like his special cocktail.)

We were in Joliet, not very far from Naperville, the destination he had originally mentioned.

"What are you delivering to Naperville?" I asked.

He didn't answer, but he did laugh.

"Is that funny?" I asked.

"Sorta," he said.

"Something illegal?" I said, trying my best to sound like I was totally at peace with delivering drugs or guns or illegal immigrants.

"Yeah, something very illegal," he said.

"Like what?"

"Like you," he said, and he laughed again.

CHAPTER 60

"WHAT THE hell are you talking about?" I asked.

"You're one of those guys who think 'cause I *sound* stupid I actually *am* stupid. But you got it all wrong."

I had some idea where this little conversation was heading, and I wasn't happy to be participating in it. Especially when I heard the locks on both sides of the cab click shut.

"I know exactly who you are," Kenny said.

The truck driver's voice transformed from street-punk nasty into something just a little smoother.

"Here's how stupid I am. I'm stupid enough to listen to the radio and all the news announcements about the cops trying to catch you. I know a lot. I know that your name is something like Jacob Brady. And I know that you're the dude everybody's looking for. And I know that I could make myself a few pieces o' gold when I turn you in."

Options automatically began clicking through my head. If I tried to fight this guy, we'd end up in a sure-to-be-head-on highway collision, even if I had the smallest chance of taking the wheel from him and knocking him out. This was no road movie.

My next option was that I could try to bullshit my way out of the situation. I thought I'd give this option a shot.

"Man, I'm an out-of-work floor layer trying to get to see my girlfriend in New York. I sure am not any Jacob Brady."

He smiled at me.

"I know you're not Jacob Brady," he said. "Your name is Jacob Brandeis. I thought I'd screw with you a little."

I would be a jerk to keep playing possum with Kenny on this one. He was right. He may not have been particularly eloquent, but he certainly was not stupid.

"I'm curious, Mr. George-Jacob-Brady-Brandeis," he said. "What in hell did you do to get the folks at the Store so goddamn pissed off?"

I was silent for at least sixty seconds.

"Huh? What is it you did?" Kenny asked.

I was ready to answer. "I tried to tell the truth."

Now he was quiet.

"You're kind of a crazy mother, ain't you?" Kenny said.

"I don't mean to preach," I said. "But I just don't think that telling the truth is all that crazy."

"I guess I agree. But I'm still not buying you, man. The Store? They're gonna hang you when they get you."

"You're probably right," I said. "I'm going to get hanged for writing a book."

I slipped my hand into my jeans pocket. The little lump of a flash drive—my past, my present, my future—

felt so stupid and unimportant next to my key chain, a box of Tic Tacs, and a few coins.

"You *wrote a book?* I just assumed you did something like kill some big shot at New Burg headquarters or that you messed with Tom Owens's wife."

"No. All's I did…" *Why was I starting to sound like Kenny?* "All's I did was write down the sneaky shit they do at the Store. How they weasel their way into people's lives. How they contol what you do, what you buy, maybe even what you think."

"A book," Kenny said. He shook his head. "That's amazing."

I thought, perhaps foolishly, that I heard a note of understanding in his voice, but I was wrong. He kept shaking his head in wonderment.

Then he added, "Amazing. It's goddamn amazing. Who the hell would want to read a book about that?" A pause. Then he said, "Shit. Who the hell would even want to read *a book?*"

CHAPTER 61

I PRETENDED to be asleep, as if pretending to be asleep were a plan in and of itself. I pretended to snore quietly, as if sleeping and snoring quietly were also part of the plan. But there was no plan. A not-so-dumbass teenager was my ultimate downfall. Who would have predicted that?

"I know you're not really sleeping, Jacob ol' buddy," Kenny said. "I got a girl who does the same thing. She pretends to be sleepin' and snorin' when she doesn't want to play around."

My response was simple: "Son of a bitch."

"There's a rest stop right up here," Kenny said. "I'm going to pull over before we haul in to Naperville. My bladder isn't what it used to be."

The rest stop was nothing but three unusable phone booths and a few weak streetlights. It was deserted and depressing.

"Now, here's how we've got to do this. I'm gonna lock the doors behind me, and then I'm gonna stand right next to your door and take a leak. Just in case you get rambunctious and decide that you can knock me over and take off. That would just be foolish."

So Kenny did what he said he would do. In fact he leaned his back against my door while he relieved himself. Then he motioned for me to lower my window. I pantomimed back that I couldn't. I mouthed the words *electric window*. Kenny nodded. He scooted around to his side, unlocked the truck, and slid into the driver's seat.

"I was thinking," he said. "You got a name for it?"

"Of course. It's called *Twenty-Twenty*."

"I get it. You're a clever bastard, ain't you?"

"Not that clever," I said. "I'm going to Naperville with you."

"*Twenty-Twenty*," he repeated, as if he hadn't heard me speak. There was a long pause. Kenny looked ahead at the weeds and trees beyond the filthy phone booths and overflowing trash cans. Then he turned and looked at me.

"Get outta the truck," he said.

"No. I don't need . . ."

"Get outta the truck," he repeated.

He clicked open the locked doors.

"Go ahead," Kenny said as he started the truck engine.

I opened the door and slid down off my seat and onto the ground. Then I turned around and looked at Kenny.

"*Twenty-Twenty*," he said. "I think I may just read *that* book."

The truck took off.

CHAPTER 62

IN JOLIET, Illinois, I hopped a freight train.

That's right. I hopped a freight train. Suddenly I was living in a folk song.

In this Store-controlled techno-packed world, where the sky was covered with drones and supersonic planes, freight trains still existed. And when I saw a guy hoist himself from a ditch alongside the tracks onto a big red car marked NYC PENN STATION, I followed him on board.

After twelve hours of inhaling the overwhelming odor of pig feces, keeping an eye on two fellow travelers who, I knew, would gladly slit my throat to steal my wallet, and eating a Subway sandwich with shredded lettuce that had turned brown around three days ago, I was in New York City.

Twenty minutes later I was somewhere on West 24th Street and Tenth Avenue. Between a bodega and a Chinese restaurant was a FedEx store, and fifteen dollars later my cherished flash drive had been transformed into good old hard copy—a four-hundred-and-ten-page manuscript. I bought a cardboard box, slipped the pages inside, and asked the clerk to tie it with string.

I was nervous. I was exhausted. I was hungry as hell. I didn't even give a crap when the middle-aged woman behind the FedEx counter thought it was perfectly okay to say, "Hey, mister, have you considered taking a shower? You stink."

I was out of there and headed downtown to SoHo, to Anne Gutman's office. The drones were beginning to hover. The stress was making me light-headed. Although I had been to Anne Gutman's office around thirty times, I was having trouble remembering the precise address.

I wandered off course a bit, and I worried a lot. I would have been naive to believe that the Store had given up their search for me. In fact, their efforts had most likely intensified.

If I needed something to scare me even more, it was at that precise moment that I heard a woman on the sidewalk say, "That's gotta be him. That's the guy. Jacob Brandeis."

It was also the precise moment when I recognized that I was standing in front of the building that housed Anne's office.

Here goes everything.

CHAPTER 63

A FEW hours pass, and my life consists of waiting for Anne Gutman's opinion on my manuscript. I am waiting as a man accused of mass murder waits for a jury decision. I can think of nothing else—not the thousands of people searching for me, not the consequences of my possible capture. I think my book is really important. Now I need Anne Gutman to think so, too.

But she's not calling, and I realize that I'm living on nothing but luck—good luck and bad luck. There was Maggie Pine; that was good luck. There was Kenny at the start of my truck ride; that was very bad luck. Then there was Kenny at the end of my truck ride; that was unbelievably good luck.

Anne gave me two fifty-dollar bills when I left her office in my stinky state of anxiety and manic fear. If you want to know what kind of Manhattan hotel lodging you can get for less than a hundred bucks (with a little left over for a nine-dollar sandwich and two Heinekens), I can tell you this: I'm staying in a place on Twelfth Avenue called...get ready for this...HOTEL. That's it. That's the name. Not HOTEL WEST SIDE, not LARRY'S HOTEL, not ECONOMY LODGING. No, just HOTEL, and it looks exactly what you think a place called HOTEL should look like: not just the flaking paint stained with fluids you don't want to think about, but also bedsheets and a dirty towel that clearly haven't been replaced in a few days, maybe a few weeks.

A shower helps. It helps as much as lukewarm water and a sliver of used soap can possibly help. It washes away the stink and the dirt and the grease and the sweat. But nothing can wash away the fear of something that could go wrong mixed with the hope that everything might turn out just fine.

Eleven dollars of Anne Gutman's money purchases a disposable phone. I bought it from an African guy who was displaying his merchandise on a sidewalk. But I knew the damn thing worked. As soon as I bought it I called Anne, left my temporary number on her machine, and told her to call me ("Please, please, please, call me, for Christ's sake. I'm living a horror story. I need to know what's happening").

By midnight—after I had spent way too much time with Jimmy Fallon and Seth Meyers and Charlie Rose—no Anne, no call.

I call her again and again, and all I ever hear is "You've reached Anne Gutman. I can't come to..."

I turn off the television. I lie on the filthy bed. I hold the disposable cell phone in my hand as if it were a religious object given to me by Jesus Christ.

Just before 4:00 a.m., my friend the phone and I take a walk to a liquor store, the kind of liquor store that has a bulletproof shield in front of all the bottles and a bulletproof booth where the owner takes your cash and completes your transaction.

Call me, Anne. Call me, Anne. Call me, Anne, for Christ's sake. This puts the march in my steps.

I buy a pint of Heaven Hill bourbon and a package of barbecue-flavored Pringles. I walk back to HOTEL.

Call me, Anne. Call me, Anne. Call me…

By 7:00 a.m., no phone call, no Anne, no bourbon, no Pringles…no hope.

CHAPTER 64

WHAT THE hell should I do now?

I'm afraid to walk the streets for fear of being spotted. I have definitely moved into crazyland. Even though I'm certain that they've got surveillance cameras in my rat hole, I can't actually find any. But looking for them— standing on the squeaky bed, kneeling on the broken dresser—kills some time.

I sneak down to Anne's office, in SoHo. Her assistants both say that Ms. Gutman is in Houston on business. ("We've given her your messages.") I am about to head to the elevator when one of the women says, "Oh, Ms. Gutman said to give you this." She hands me four fifty-dollar bills. Maybe I could make a nice living waiting for Anne Gutman.

I go back to HOTEL. Staying in that room makes me sadder than anyone deserves to be. Drinking cheap bourbon, eating cold burgers, and watching those bickering broads on *The View* is not the life I had planned for myself. Lonely? I think only dead people are lonelier than I am. I don't know for sure what it's like to be dead, but I sure as shit am standing mighty close.

I go into one of those chain drugstores near Times Square. Walgreens? Duane Reade? CVS? Who the hell knows? I buy a disposable razor, store-brand ibuprofen, store-brand shaving cream, and a Hershey's Special Dark chocolate bar (the giant size).

I go up to the cashier, a sweet-looking Latina no older than eighteen.

"How you doing today, sir?" she says. I'm thinking, *Is this New York, or have I clicked my heels and gone back to Nebraska?* (Yeah, I know it's supposed to be Kansas, but my life is in Nebraska.)

"I'm doing fine. How about you?"

She's ringing up the purchases with exceptional speed. Total, $11.47, and "Sure, I would like to make a one-dollar donation to the Children's Diabetes Fund."

She hands me back a few dollar bills and coins in change. Outside, I go to stuff it in my pocket and I realize that in among the paper money she handed me is a business card. It's blank except for four handwritten words: CHECK YOUR TEXT MESSAGES.

I run back into the store. The girl behind the counter is gone. I stand in front of an endcap display of skin moisturizer.

I punch into my messages as fast as I can. In those few seconds I think it might be Anne or even Megan or some thug from the store or . . . there's the text:

Hey, J, check out "The Store for Books" page. Very cool.

My sweaty fingers move faster than ever. I move to

Google. Then Google moves me to the landing page of the Store. Just below the bullshit banners selling toaster ovens and Lego and plus-size bathing suits is this:

The book the world's been waiting for . . .
Twenty-Twenty
The blockbuster that's bound to bust the Store wide open

CHAPTER 65

BACK AT HOTEL, I click on the little line that says: "Read all about it. Now!" The screen fills with typography that's supposed to look like human handwriting. It says: "How can we make your life better today?"

I know Megan's username (Major345Meg) and her password (LindsAlex9#9). In a few seconds I'm on the "Books, E-Readers, Audio" page. My index finger is actually sweating. My hands are shaking. I feel as if I'm about to push the button that will start a nuclear war.

In a way I could be right about that. This is either the beginning or the end of my own personal crazy nuclear war.

Boom! There it is!

*The gutsy exposé of the world's most
important and influential website
Behind the scenes at the Store
An anonymous author tells the truth
about the world's best-known company*

Twenty-Twenty
Enter the incredible world of the Store

My hands shake even more as I push the Download button. Within thirty seconds the words DOWNLOAD COMPLETED fill the screen. I move to chapter 1, page 7. It is a headache-making, eye-aching chore to try to read the small type on the crappy little disposable phone screen. I constantly need to enlarge the type and then reduce it in order to move on to the next paragraph.

But hey, who gives a good goddamn? This is *Twenty-Twenty*. This is incredible.

So what do I find?

This isn't my book at all.

These aren't my words.

My name isn't even on the cover.

Holy shit. It's not my book. And I'm no author.

This fraud is an epic windblast of praise to the genius of the Store.

This is a disgusting ode to the brilliance of Thomas P. Owens. The manuscript even keeps referring to him as "our beloved founder."

I rush pages and chapters ahead. No matter where my eyes land, it is a totally ridiculous piece of bullshit. I read how the Store has "made America a better place to live because it's given America a better place to shop."

According to this version, the Store is not interested in making a profit for at least another fifteen years (bull-shit!). The Store underprices every item they sell—from prescription drugs to lawn mowers to disposable diapers to finely crafted Stickley furniture (bullshit!). The Store believes in full discretion and privacy for all their customers. "Without the trust of our consumer partners we have no business" (double bullshit!).

I begin scrolling with fierce speed. Perhaps every fifteen pages I recognize a sentence from my original manuscript. Usually it's a harmless sentence like: "And this was just part of Thomas P. Owens's dream."

I leave the book itself and move to a page entitled "What Do Other Customers Think of This Book? Read the Ratings from A+ to F."

Here's a challenge for the Store. This must be the most hated book in America.

One customer writes: "In a few words: this book stinks. A boring valentine. *F* as in phony. *F* as in foolish. *F* as in freaking stupid."

Another customer says: "I guess the author was ashamed to put his name on this piece of garbage. I don't blame him or her."

I lie on the smelly HOTEL bed. I close my eyes. And then...then I sit up in bed as if the room is on fire.

I smile. The smile grows bigger. The smile turns into laughter. The laughter is unstoppable.

I'm tired and sleepy.

Yet I leap out of bed.

I stomp my legs and feet like a crazy little kid.

It worked! The Store published the stupid bogus version of my book.

CHAPTER 66

"HAVE WE heard anything?" the old man says.

"Nothing yet, sir," says the serious-looking young woman in brown canvas shorts and hiking boots. She carries a tan Osprey backpack. A single earphone is attached to her left ear. She is the old man's executive assistant, and she is seldom more than a few feet from his side.

The old man—perhaps he is nearing eighty—is in remarkably fine shape. Everyone in his entourage says so. He is tall and stands straight. His white beard is closely trimmed, and his gray hair is full and thick.

The old man flew by private jet last night to Flagstaff. This morning he is hiking the hills near Supai on the periphery of Grand Canyon National Park. He's not at all alone, however. His entourage includes the executive assistant, two mountain hiking guides, the old man's fifty-year-old son, and the old man's thirty-three-year-old wife. There is also a camp cook (well, a chef-nutritionist, actually), a tech support man, and the old man's personal physician.

"Call New Burg. I want to know what's happening," the old man says. His manner is strong but not unpleasant. He's so used to being rich and in charge that there's no need for him to be anything less than gracious. "Now!" he says sternly.

"Don't have to call, sir. New Burg is calling *us*," the assistant says. As she pushes a few buttons to accept the message, he looks over the mountains above and below him. The red and brown and yellow and coral palette stuns him with its beauty. He thinks what he frequently thinks: *I'm a lucky man*. No one would argue with that.

"I'll take the message myself," he says to the executive assistant. She hands him the earphone, and he holds it close.

"What's the story?" he asks.

The caller says, "It's over. A big nothing. Done and done."

"Hah!" the old man says, then adds, "Not even a hiccup. Just a book. It's a stupid e-book.

"Can you imagine?" he says as he hands the earphone back to his assistant, "Just a book."

Thomas P. Owens begins to laugh. He looks out over the mountains. He owns thousands of acres of this land. A shiver of warmth rushes through him. The beloved founder's laugh grows louder. The colors of the mountains grow more intense.

His lovely wife touches his shoulder. His physician keeps a steady eye on him. His executive assistant replaces the earphone on her ear. The personal chef begins unpacking lunch.

He owns so much land in this area. Not merely the land he is standing on, but also so much land beyond that and then beyond that and . . .

His laughter winds down, and he speaks. His voice is firm and hearty and happy.

"Not even a hiccup. A book. The thing is just a book."

He takes a big gulp of water from the bottle that his beautiful young wife has handed him.

"I'd like to hike a bit more before we have lunch," the old man says.

Nobody dares disagree with him. A few of them wipe dirt and sweat from their faces. A few of them drink some water. They are about to begin.

"I'll have everything ready when you return, sir," the chef-nutritionist says.

"Perfect," says the old man. "Let's get going."

And then.

"Hold on just a minute, sir," his executive assistant says. "It looks like you're getting another message."

CHAPTER 67

"ARE YOU ready, Anne?"

"Completely. The question is, are *you* ready, Jacob?"

"I've only dreamed of a day like this day most of my life," I say.

We are standing in a small room in a large conference space on Wooster Street, in SoHo. Anne and I are about to—I can't believe I'm lucky enough to be saying this—hold a press conference.

Word is out: the Store has published a totally counterfeit version of *Twenty-Twenty*. The real version—a tough-minded, inflammatory, scandalous book—is going to be available starting tomorrow.

In the big space on Wooster Street, a noisy menagerie of bloggers and newspaper writers and e-zine journalists has gathered. People from the *Wall Street Journal* and Vulture .com and BuzzFeed and YouTube and *Salon* and *Slate* and virtually every website and cable channel in the country.

The only media source that's missing, of course, is the Store.

A PR guy holds open the door to our waiting room. *Ladies and gentlemen, please be prepared to have your heads blown off.*

We walk toward the cameras. The crowd moves closer to the dais, where we stand before a gigantic cluster of microphones.

After a few moments of the "press" settling down, I begin to speak. I am—to my own surprise—calm. My voice feels strong and sensible.

"Good morning. I'm Jacob Brandeis." I pause. There is no applause. I'm an idiot. This is the press, not the public. I start talking again.

"We know why we're here. You know why we're here…"

Why do I keep pausing? Of course they know why they're there.

"Beginning tomorrow, the authentic, unexpurgated, *real* version of *Twenty-Twenty* will be available. The people who want to know the truth about the Store can find it on a new site called WrittenTruth.com. It will be delivered within twenty-four hours. But if you just can't wait twenty-four hours, it will also be available at whatever independent bookstores throughout the country have not yet been devoured by the Store. And if I have to, I'll stand on the back of a truck in Times Square and sell copies to anyone who wants to read them."

Some laughter. Then mostly silence.

"I know that you all have plenty of questions…"

Suddenly an explosion of hands and shouts of "Mr. Brandeis"…"Jacob"…"Mr. Brandeis"…

I hold up my hands. I talk loudly into the mike. Reverb throughout the room.

"I will be very glad to tell you in detail how we pulled this off. We'll do that some other time. But I can give you the general answer right now: exceptional people—family and friends—were secretly in on the plan from the beginning. We all acted in a way that got the Store to believe we were writing one kind of book, but in fact we were writing the book that is *now* being released.

"My great kids, Lindsay and Alex, were continually making videos of my great wife, Megan, and me arguing venomously about my project. Then they'd send that video to the Store. The Store thought the kids were cooperating, but of course all they were doing was verifying that the Store was recording us on their own surveillance cameras. The one thing the Store didn't know was this: it was all a *huge act,* a delicately planned act—and, I might add, a very scary performance. The Store believed the story we handed them: a crazy father was writing a book, and the wife and kids were so loyal to the Store that . . . well, you get it.

"As to the others who helped us pull it off . . . they're all in the book. Suffice it to say that Megan and I had recruited certain of our neighbors—Marie and Bud and Bette—to become part of the plan. Even Megan's supposedly rotten boss, Sam Reed, had some secret scores to settle with the Store management. So Sam became part of the act.

"I'll be moving offstage in a minute. I'm a writer, not an actor. But I do want to talk about two of the most amazing people behind the scenes, two women who did as much as I did to make this book happen.

"Yes, I wrote the book, the real book, the true *Twenty-Twenty,* but nothing would have been possible without the unwavering encouragement and the wildly sneaky brain of the most important and honest book publisher in the world, Anne Gutman."

I swing my left arm backward, and Anne steps closer to the microphones. Her voice is sure and strong. As my mom used to say, "You can hear her brains in her voice."

"Jacob Brandeis wrote a brilliant investigative book under essentially wartime circumstances. I was a conduit, a fan, a citizen. I am proud to have been part of it."

Anne and I hug, and now—oh, shit, my eyes are filling up with tears—I replace Anne at the microphone.

"I...I...sometimes I was so arrogant...obnoxious to her, but she never gave up...I...nineteen years ago, I...I chose right. Here's Megan."

She walks out. She looks terrific. New York all the way: black slacks and black shirt and her hair tied back with a white scarf. As we kiss—I could honestly say the kiss was passionate—Alex and Lindsay walk over to us.

"I love you," I say again and again to the three of them. I hold them so tightly that I actually think I might squeeze them until they burst.

"Yay," shouts Alex. "Group hug!"

I don't think any of us wanted that hug to end. Megan tilts her head back and looks me squarely in the eyes. Then she says, "There's just one thing I've been wanting to tell you."

"What's that?" I ask.

Tears are streaming down her cheeks.

She looks at me. She speaks.

"Ugga-bugga."

FIFTEEN MONTHS LATER

CHAPTER 68

WHEN I began writing *Twenty-Twenty* I was so fueled by anger and self-righteousness that I had no idea what I wanted to accomplish beyond exposing the Store's policies and procedures.

Yes, at times when I was writing in my stifling attic in New Burg I had the occasional fantasy that the Store would come tumbling down. But of course I knew that would never happen, and I also knew (and worried about the fact) that thousands of people depended on the Store for their livelihood and even for their very lives.

So after the book appeared, the Store did not disappear from the face of the earth. It remained an enormous factor in the United States economy, but it did do a monumental job at self-reform. I don't doubt that this reform came about quickly to prevent state and federal governments from doing the reforming. But it came about.

Listening devices, surveillance devices, and video-recording devices were removed from streets and stores and restaurants and, most important, from private homes.

Were things perfect? Of course not. There would always be people who would try to make a profit at all costs. (I'm talking to you, Thomas P. Owens.) But things were definitely better.

Bette and Bud were back in New Burg, and we e-mailed and texted back and forth quite a bit. Their observation: "The town looks the same, but it doesn't *feel* the same. It seems...better and calmer. Folks aren't looking over their shoulders all the time. We'll see what happens."

Yep. That's all we can do. We'll see.

As for the Brandeis family? Well, I can tell you this. The book did not make us rich. But it did make us—as my mother would say—comfortable enough not to worry ourselves half to death.

Megan and I were both tapped for a lot of juicy freelance assignments, and we worked hard at them. Investigative journalism was part of our mutual DNA. But so far, no subject has come along as important or provocative as the Store. I don't think anything will compare to that.

We moved back to New York City, away from our old neighborhood. We're now in SoHo. It's a lot more convenient than FiDi and close enough to Anne Gutman's office for she and I to have a standing Thursday lunch date at Balthazar (she pays).

Alex is a student at high school. He's doing very well...in tennis, soccer, and video club. The SAT tutors are lining up.

This past Thursday Megan and I drove Lindsay up to Connecticut. Alex came with us (reluctantly) to do the heavy lifting. Lindsay's starting at Wesleyan University. She'll be an English major with a minor in journalism. Surprise!

The car ride up to school was treacherous. Thunder, lightning, and lake-deep puddles on Route 66. By the time the four of us wrestled Lindsay's boxes and suitcases and that damn trunk into her dorm, we were so soaked that we didn't even bother opening umbrellas as we walked back to the car to say our good-byes.

"Hey, man, we've never been, like, so apart from each other before," Alex said to his sister. We hugged. Then we hugged some more.

"We're getting good at these group hugs," Megan said.

"That's *your* opinion," said Alex, but he did not pull away from the group.

"You know, this feels like we're four actors in a really dramatic ending of a French movie," I said.

Lindsay spoke: "There's so much rain that I can't even be sure if I'm actually crying."

There was no camouflaging the fact that both Megan and I were crying.

"In my humble opinion, I think this weather is absolutely beautiful," I said.

"You really are a crazy guy, Dad," said Alex.

"No. I'm right," I said. "Take a look. There's not a drone in the sky."

YOU CAN TAKE MICHAEL BENNETT OUT OF NEW YORK CITY, BUT YOU CAN'T TAKE THE COP OUT OF MICHAEL BENNETT . . .

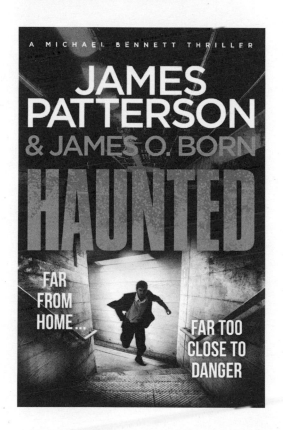

FOR AN EXCERPT, TURN THE PAGE.

I LOOKED DOWN the barrel of my Glock 19 service weapon. Lori Armstrong, a tall detective with long blond hair from the Forty-Third precinct, stood across from me. Hector Nunez, a crimes and missing-persons detective who looked like he should play linebacker for the Jets, was about to knock on the door.

We were three stories up in the dark, musty, hot hallway of an apartment building off Castle Hill Avenue near the I-278 overpass. I could feel the vibration of every semi that rumbled by.

This was an arrest I needed. I desperately wanted something to occupy my mind and satisfy my sense of justice. Some cops found refuge in their homelife. I found that it worked both ways. Right now, I needed to be at work and get some distance so I could be the man I wanted to be at home. I had to get my mind off my son Brian any way I could.

The suspect was a career dope dealer named Laszlo Montez, and I made him for a double homicide in Jackie

Robinson Park, near 153rd Street, in sight of Bethany Baptist Church. He'd used a knife on another dealer and the dealer's girlfriend. The dealer had been stabbed from behind, unaware of the threat. His girlfriend had been slashed over and over. It was messy. Senseless. The guy in this apartment was good for it. And his ass was mine.

Hector looked my way. I nodded, and he knocked. Politely at first. No sense in scaring the suspect.

A voice from inside shouted back in Spanish. *"¿Quién es?" Who is it?* Like any good NYPD detective, I had a working knowledge of basic Spanish.

Hector said, "It's me. Open up."

There wasn't even an answer from inside. That meant the game was up.

Hector said in a flat voice, *"Policía: abre la puerta."* Then in English he added, "Now."

My sergeant was in the alley behind the building in case Montez managed to navigate the ancient fire escape.

Hector shouted out, "Don't play, Laz. Open up." He waited five seconds, then kicked the front door. It splintered in half and fell in pieces onto the hard wooden floor. A cat leaped away from the door and over a ratty couch.

I darted in first, my pistol up. Lori came in behind me. I scanned the shitty little apartment quickly. Bedroom, bathroom, nothing.

The window was open, and I muttered "Shit" as I wedged myself onto the fire-escape landing. It was a long way down. Cops with a thing about heights shouldn't climb around on fire escapes. But there was no choice. Montez was already a floor down and jumping onto an adjacent apartment's fire escape. Then he swung down to the second floor. I followed as Lori alerted the sergeant to be ready.

Montez was young and nimble. I was older, and, well, no one ever called me nimble. As soon as he saw me, he did the unexpected. He kicked in a window and dove into an apartment. Immediately I heard screaming. A moment later, I was in the apartment behind him.

A heavy woman wearing some kind of shower cap screamed in Spanish. By the front door, Montez stood with a knife to the throat of a teenage girl with long dark hair. She was shaking like a wet dog in January.

Montez said, "Get back. I'll cut her." He flicked the knife, and a cut opened on the girl's slender neck. A trickle of blood ran down to her white blouse. The girl let out a yelp.

My gun stayed on target. His face in the front sight. He backed to the door. The woman in the corner screamed, and a bead of sweat rolled into my left eye. I started to time my breathing. His head ducked behind the girl's face every few seconds. I felt my finger tighten on the trigger.

Then the door burst open behind him. Lori and Hector had their guns on him as well. Montez turned to face them. This time his voice cracked as he shouted, "Get back or I'll slit her throat."

His back was to me, so I acted. He had threatened a kid. She couldn't have been more than fifteen. I was pissed.

I silently holstered my pistol and stepped forward quickly. I used my left hand to block the knife from the girl's throat, then I put Montez in an arm bar. I misjudged it slightly and felt the knife bite into my hand, slicing my palm as I wrenched him away from the girl.

Lori yanked the girl to safety.

Now it was just this asshole and me. I looked to see where the knife had landed and was shocked to see it was still stuck in my hand. Holy shit.

That was it. I threw a right cross and watched as Montez stumbled back. Then I jerked the four-inch blade from my hand. Before he regained his footing, my right knee connected with Montez's head. He was on the floor, and I fell on top of him. A two-hundred-pound sledgehammer. Then I just started to throw elbows and fists into his face. Blood splattered everywhere. Some his, some mine. I needed this. Therapy. What the hell—I was only human.

Then I heard someone shout, "Mike!" I felt a strong hand on my wrist. My sergeant pulled me away.

I looked down at what I had done. Shocked as anyone. I could've ended this with a single punch. I had lost it.

My sergeant said, "Jesus, Mike. We got him."

I looked past my raw, bloodied hands at the pulp of this punk's face. This wasn't how I operated. I was embarrassed. Ashamed.

My sergeant said, "Stand down, Mike. In fact, after you have that hand taken care of, go home. Stay there. I'll handle this. You've got enough problems to deal with at home."

Unfortunately, Sarge was right.

I FUMBLED WITH the pancake batter because of the stitches in my hand. The Bennett household kitchen wasn't small, but this morning it felt like I was on top of Mary Catherine as we whipped up enough to feed all ten kids. Wait a minute. Nine kids.

Somehow the eight-room apartment on the Upper West Side seemed empty, even with eleven people in it. The quiet was unsettling. It'd been like this for days.

Mary Catherine laid her head on my shoulder as a show of support, but all it did was remind me how bad things could get. Once I had two plates ready for serving, I forced a smile. I burst out of the kitchen and said, "Who's the hungriest?"

Usually this would elicit a battle between kids going after the first of the food. Today I got no response. None. Then Trent and Eddie motioned me over like hipsters trying to be cool in a trendy restaurant.

After I set the plates down, I winked at Chrissy and pinched her nose. I would have given anything to have one of her smiles at the moment. She tried, God help her. She showed her teeth, but it wasn't the usual breathtaking spectacle of a little girl's sincere show of happiness.

I shuffled back into the kitchen to return to work. That was the only way to stay sane for the moment.

Mary Catherine had more plates ready, but I just stood there like I had forgotten my job. Like I had lost my purpose.

I looked at Mary Catherine's blond hair as strands tumbled onto her shoulder. She had told me she learned to focus by helping her mom feed three brothers and two younger sisters. She was made for this. I still remembered our first awkward meeting, when she showed up after corresponding with my late wife, Maeve. She came directly from Dublin and just stared at me as I informed her we had ten kids. Ten. But she never faltered. Even in the face of my grandfather Seamus, who thought I brought her in to replace him. It didn't take long for the lovely young Irish girl to win over my surly grandfather.

That was all in my darkest time. Maeve was in the last days of her fight with cancer, and I was lost. Somehow I had survived.

Now I was trying to figure out how to face dark times again.

THE KIDS MADE their usual assembly line to clean up the breakfast plates, with Juliana and Jane acting as supervisors. Those two had CEO written all over them. I could hardly believe my little girls were such beautiful young women who didn't shy away from responsibility. If you added Mary Catherine to the mix, you could say that women had kept me alive and functioning for many years.

Mary Catherine worked on getting the youngest kids' backpacks and lunches together. It was seamless. And I stood in the corner, almost useless. Mary Catherine looked up and winked at me. How had this lass from Ireland gone from the kids' nanny to my love in a few short years? My heart broke a little bit when I thought about what the family had to deal with now, but this was not the time to give up or abandon my job as a father.

I clapped my hands together and said, "Okay, gang. I'm going to bring the bus around front. Three minutes, and the Bennetts renew their assault on civilization."

That got a smile from Bridget. That was enough for me.

The short ride to the kids' school, Holy Name, was silent at first. Everyone sat like zombies in the twelve-passenger Ford Super Duty van. It had years on it, but not that many miles. I remember the look on the car sales-man's face when I proved I could fill the van with just my own kids. It was a stretch financially then. Now it was a necessity. A fact of our daily life.

The kids were seated with the youngest in the back, as always. Poor Chrissy and Shawna would never move up until someone went to college. Just thinking about that and the fact that college was not in Brian's future right now made me want to cry.

Eddie said, "When will Brian come home?"

Ah, my Einstein always knew which question was most important. I took a moment to form my answer and said, "Well, buddy, I just don't know." *Real helpful, Dad.*

Ricky said, "I thought you knew all about that kind of stuff."

"I wish I knew more. What's important is that we put Brian in our prayers and he knows how much he's missed."

Fiona started to sniffle. It was a precursor to crying, and that would cause a ripple effect throughout the van. I'd seen it too many times already. I had to do something fast.

I shouted, "Look!"

All heads turned to the right and looked out on West 96th Street, where I was staring.

Jane said, "What do you see, Dad?"

"I think it's Derek Jeter."

"Where?" came a chorus.

"Right there in front of the Gristedes supermarket." I pointed at a huge man in a blue Brooks Brothers suit with his flab poking out around his belt. "Looks like he's put on a little weight since retirement."

Trent wailed, "Noooooo! That's not Jeter." He followed the Yankees better than he followed any of the classes he was in.

"Are you sure?"

Now there were some giggles as little voices said, "Not Jeter." That turned into a chant. "Not Jeter, not Jeter, not Jeter."

We pulled up to Holy Name, on Amsterdam Avenue. I knew I had survived another morning. For a change we were on time and got to see what it looked like when we weren't racing to beat the final bell and shoo the kids in before the door was locked. Sister Sheilah even waved to me.

As each kid filed out, giving me a quick hug, I felt Brian's absence like a missing limb.

I PARKED THE van in Queens and took advantage of the bus to Rikers Island. I'd been to New York City's main detention facility dozens of times before, but today it felt grim. The narrow bridge from Queens to the island in the East River made me anxious. The island itself is a giant facility where people booked on crimes from misdemeanors to homicides are processed. Today I got off in front of the main building, having used my connections to make things move quickly. There were several buildings in the facility, which could hold as many as fifteen thousand prisoners at any one time. I was told to go to a building near the front of the complex.

This main building housed males in pretrial status. Many of them were poor and couldn't afford bail. Others, like Brian, had been denied bail altogether. Our lawyer had already told me that the district attorney's office would be tough. For them, this was a chance to change the media narrative about the racist judicial system. They

12

were charging him as an adult. My little boy was considered an adult this one wretched time.

My throat was dry as I cut away from the miserable little crowd that got off the bus. They shuffled to the main visiting entrance while I moved to the side, where I was supposed to meet an old friend. Even the bright sunshine couldn't give the jail any kind of pleasant facade.

I nodded when I saw the lieutenant who had already been wildly helpful. "Hey, Vinny. I appreciate the assist."

The pudgy middle-aged bald man said, "No problem, Mike. I'm a dad, too. I know this has got to be tough on you."

I said, "Is he doing okay?"

"I just saw him, and he looked fine. You know this place is no summer camp."

He led me through a side door to a tiny room that contained only two institutional metal chairs. There was no Plexiglas. No phones or surveillance cameras. This wasn't an interview room. It was probably a place where corrections officers could get away from the stress for a few minutes. This guy was really helping me out. A rare perk of being one of New York's finest.

I stood silently in the ten-foot-by-ten-foot room; it had bland two-tone beige walls and no windows. The door opened, and Brian stood there, wearing a simple orange jumpsuit and black flip-flops. He sprang forward and gave me a hug.

The uniformed corrections officer gave me a bob of his head and backed out of the room tactfully.

I held my boy. The young man I had raised. Nursed

through the flu. Tutored in math. Taught to love sports. I held my boy, who was now facing up to ten years in the New York State prison system. I held him and started to cry.

Finally we both plopped into the two lonely chairs and just stared at each other. Was this our new normal?

Brian's eyes were bloodshot, and he had a light stubble on his face—like a tiny sparse forest. Christ—he only started shaving a year ago.

I focused and said, "Look, Brian, we're doing all we can. You've talked to the attorney. She's the best. A former ADA."

He just nodded.

I didn't want to get into the *why* of what he did. Status? Money? Who cares? I never made that much as a cop, but we had everything we needed. More than once I wondered if Brian's crime had something to do with the loss of his mother years ago. Maeve's memory still affected me every day, no matter what I was doing. Even after falling in love again. Who knows what it did to the kids, no matter how open we were with each other?

I just couldn't believe it. What had happened to Brian? My son, arrested for selling drugs. Both meth and a new form of ecstasy. It was almost too much to process.

I hadn't lectured or yelled. He knew what a terrible mistake he'd made. He realized what could happen. Now I needed answers. I had to get to the bottom of this and save him. It didn't matter to me if he wanted to be saved or not.

I said, "You've got to help us. Help yourself. I need to know who gave you that shit to sell."

He just stared at me. There was no answer. Barely an acknowledgment.

"And right there near Holy Name. The kids..." I caught myself. I channeled my inner Joe Friday. *Just the facts, ma'am.* I gave it thirty seconds. Half a minute of dead silence in this tiny room. The chilling sounds of the lockup drifting inside. Cell doors slamming. Men yelling insults back and forth. For the first time in my career, it was depressing to me.

Finally, I calmly said, "Who gave you the drugs?"

Brian's voice cracked as he said, "I'm sorry, Dad. I can't tell you." He was resolute.

My world crashed down around me.

BRIAN AND I were done for the day. There was nothing left to say. He wasn't going to tell me what I needed to know. It could've been stupid stubborn teenage pride. Acting like a tough guy, or, more likely, fear of what would happen if he talked. That was relatively new in the culture cops operated in. The whole "snitches get stitches" attitude had popped up in inner-city neighborhoods and spread through music and TV shows. Now it seemed to be the mantra of anyone under thirty.

When the door opened, I had to snatch one more hug from my son. He wrapped his arms around me as well. Then I watched silently as a corrections officer led him away. He moved like a robot. His feet shuffling and the flip-flops making a sad slapping sound on the concrete floor.

I headed toward the exit, where my friend Vinny was waiting to lead me out. I said, "Is there anything you can do to protect him?"

He smiled and patted me on the shoulder. "We have

Brian in what we call the nerd ward. Hackers and financial guys who decided they weren't going to follow the rules. Those sorts of perps. He only comes into contact with the general population if he goes out to exercise once a week or if we have to move people around because of trouble. But I promise, Mike, we're keeping a close eye on him."

This was special treatment because I was a cop. I wasn't going to refuse it.

When he told me Brian was safe for now, I thought I'd break down and cry right in front of him.

What did people without friends working in the jail do? What about people with no access to a decent lawyer? It made me think about cases I had worked and how I would persuade people to cooperate. Now I saw that they often had no other choice.

Then Vinny took my arm, and as we started to walk, he leaned in closer and said, "The rumor is that the DA's office wants to make an example of Brian. Wants to show that they'll go after a white kid as hard as a black kid. And they want to look fair by not showing preference to a cop's son."

I wasn't sure I wanted to hear the truth like that all at once. It felt like a punch in the gut. I slapped the cinderblock wall in frustration. The jolt of pain through my body reminded me that I had stitches in that hand. Blood stained the white bandage.

Vinny draped his arm over my shoulder and subtly headed us toward the exit.

I found myself shuffling, just like Brian. I wondered if it had something to do with this place.

This place I would never look at the same way again.

WHEN I LEFT the jail, I knew exactly what I had to do. By the time I got back to my van in Queens, clouds had drifted in and given the streets a particularly gloomy look. I couldn't go in to the office. I was on leave. Officially for my injury, but unofficially for beating the murder suspect Laszlo Montez. Thank God no one asked too many questions about a guy who put a knife to a teenage girl's throat and murdered two people.

My sergeant told me to just go with it. There might be an investigation later, but for now I was a hero who'd been stabbed by a murder suspect. The city sure didn't care much about heroes' kids.

But I was still a cop. And, much more important, a father.

Like any cop worth his salt, I had informants. The word *snitch* had fallen out of favor in police work over the last few years. But it's hard to find words that rhyme with *informant*. "Snitches get stitches" is catchier than something like "Informants get dormant."

Informants are a fact of police work. People like to point out all the problems with using informants, but few understand the benefits. They can go places cops can't. Cops can't be everywhere at once. Informants help in that effort. They also give insight into how a criminal thinks.

Jodie Foster didn't need Anthony Hopkins's help in *The Silence of the Lambs* because his character was a Boy Scout. He was a psychopath, and he found the break in the case. Informants are vital and horrible at the same time. And cops need them no matter how they feel about them.

I knew people. Some through favors and some through fear. Both seemed to work well. My biggest issue was that whoever gave Brian that shit was somewhere near Holy Name. At least that's where he was operating. I had to be discreet.

My first stop was at a deli—or, more precisely, behind a deli—off La Salle Street. I ditched the van and walked to the alley behind the North Side Deli. After just a few minutes, a skinny white guy with a shaved head and tats up and down both arms stepped out for a smoke.

He didn't notice me until I said, "Hello, Walter." It was satisfying to see him jump. "You could pass for either a skinhead or a chemo patient. You need to eat a little more while you're at work."

The young man turned and said, "No labels, man. I just like short hair now. Besides, some of my beliefs don't go over so well inside."

I didn't have time to waste. I said, "I need information."

"I'm clean. You got nothing on me."

"I don't *need* anything on you. The statute hasn't run out on the guy you stabbed over near Riverside Park."

"That was self-defense. You even said he was just a dope dealer. I already paid that debt. I told you about the West Side gang's gun stash."

"You paid part of your debt. Now I need more. Unless you want the judge to decide what, exactly, is self-defense and what's just a senseless attack."

"But the guy wasn't even hurt bad. A few stitches, a little blood. Who cares?"

I looked down at my bandaged hand and said, "I bet he cares. And I still have his contact info."

Walter looked resigned as his head dipped. He mumbled, "What do you need to know?"

"Who's giving meth and X to local kids to sell?"

"Man, this ain't my neighborhood. It's none of my business."

"Make it your business."

Walter caught my tone and looked up at me. "This means something to you, doesn't it?"

I gave him a silent stare.

He said, "You'll owe me."

I just nodded.

"Big-time."

I said, "Don't push it, Walter, or some of your white supremacist asshole buddies might find out that your real last name is Nussbaum."

I knew he'd do as I said.

I SPREAD THE love for ten blocks in every direction. By midnight I'd be a curse on the tongue of every dealer and informant on the Upper West Side.

I spoke with Lenny Whitehead, a black crack dealer whose daughter I once rescued from a gang he owed money to. Back then he'd offered to kill anyone I wanted him to. I thought it was a joke, but I didn't want to push it.

Manny Garcia, a slick former Latin King, talked to me because I'd helped him when he was fingered for a homicide he didn't commit. I found the real killer, and Manny had been my best friend ever since.

Billy Haskins, a former set designer I put away for selling coke to Broadway actors, talked because he didn't want any trouble. The little Bostonian had no use for New Yorkers other than as drug customers or producers willing to pay union scale.

Everyone was part of the program. I'd have answers soon.

All the social interaction with lowlifes had made me

late to pick up the kids. When I pulled the van into the pickup lane, I saw my brood lined up along the fence talking with Sister Sheilah. That was never a good sign.

I rolled to a stop and hopped out, knowing the best defense is a good offense. Whatever Sister Sheilah was asking, I was prepared to answer.

I was shocked when she smiled at me. I wasn't sure exactly what she was doing at first, because I'd seen her smile so rarely. I stammered, "S-sorry I'm a little late."

She said, "Ten minutes is a little late. Forty-five makes me worried you'd forgotten you had kids."

Was that a joke? I was too terrified to ask.

The sister said, "It's no problem, Mr. Bennett. Bridget and I were discussing the fine points of bedazzling and other crafts." She stepped toward me and led me by the arm away from the children as they started to file into the van. In a low voice she said, "We've been so worried about Brian. Anything new?"

"No, Sister. Not yet. There's a long way to go."

"We'll pray for him and for you."

"Thank you, Sister. I need prayers right about now."

Once we were back home, I opened the door to a smell that made me smile. It was one of Mary Catherine's standards. It took me a minute to pinpoint the aroma. Irish pot roast with brown gravy. I caught the look on each kid's face as he or she crossed the threshold. Sometimes it's the little things that can perk you up.

Mary Catherine came out of the kitchen looking like a young housewife from the fifties. A white apron, a smile, and a twinkle in her eyes.

She said, "Dinner in two hours. Two hours of hard labor. Homework first. The chores next. Cleanup last, and in that order." She looked across the room, and for the first time I noticed my grandfather Seamus standing in the corner, looking out at the street below. She said to him, "You're in charge of homework. Make yourself useful if you want to be fed."

I doubted she had ever spoken that way to a priest when she lived in Tipperary or Dublin. But it was hard to think of my grandfather as a priest unless he was wearing his clerical collar. And sometimes even then it was hard to believe. But despite his impish and mischievous nature, he had been a blessing to me since my childhood. And now he was here for my children.

I WATCHED THE miracle of dinner at the Bennett house unfold. Mary Catherine was the author of this blessed event, and I couldn't express how much I appreciated her efforts to keep the kids' lives normal. She awed me. By dinnertime, the kids had their homework done, their chores completed, and the table set.

Once again the crowd was quiet. The empty chair where Brian normally sat didn't help matters.

Seamus, sitting at the far end of the table from me, bowed his head, as he did before each meal. The kids followed his lead. He said in a low, comforting voice, "Lord, thank you for our many blessings. Thank you for our time together. Thank you for allowing us to realize how fleeting it can be. Please bless this family and protect our precious Brian. Amen."

A quiet chorus of "Amen" followed.

Dinner proceeded with the clank of silverware and the occasional comment just to break the silence. Mary Catherine engaged Chrissy. She was our best chance if we wanted to hear a quirky, funny story from the day.

Mary Catherine said, "What did you learn in history today, Chrissy?"

Usually the little girl would light up at a chance to tell a story in front of the whole family. Instead she mumbled, "We talked about the men in Boston who decided we shouldn't be part of England anymore."

Mary Catherine took a moment and managed to gather everyone's attention without saying a word. Then she said, "Listen, everyone. I know we're worried about Brian. You can believe your father is doing everything he can to help him. But sometimes things don't work out the way we expect them to. Not better, not worse—just not like we expect."

Now she was playing to the crowd's full attention.

"My brother Ken wanted to come to America. He's a big, burly lad and a great fan of the Kennedys. All he talked about was coming to Boston. But he got in trouble."

Shawna said, "What kind of trouble?" We were all hooked.

"It was a bar fight, and Ken punched a man who hit his head when he fell on the floor. My brother was charged with assault and later convicted. He didn't have to go to jail, but he had a conviction on his record, and that kept him from doing what he expected to do. That conviction kept him from coming to America. But you know what?"

Chrissy and Bridget both said, "What?"

"Things turned out differently for him. He met a lovely

girl. And now he lives right there in Dublin with two beautiful kids. He has a good job and is happier than he could ever think of being. It's different from what he expected, but certainly not worse. Sometimes things happen in life, and we just have to accept them."

I could almost see the kids understanding what she was saying and feeling better. It felt like the pace of eating even picked up. But Seamus was still quiet. None of his usual silly quips or semi-risqué jokes. When I looked at him, I could see why. He was silently crying, trying to hide it from the kids.

JAMES PATTERSON
BOOK**SHOTS**

stories at the speed of life

BOOK**SHOTS** are page-turning stories by James Patterson and other writers that can be read in one sitting.

Each and every one is fast-paced, 100% story-driven; a shot of pure entertainment guaranteed to satisfy.

Under 150 pages
Under £3

Available as new, compact paperbacks, ebooks and audio, everywhere books are sold.

For more details, visit: **www.bookshots.com**

BOOK**SHOTS**
THE ULTIMATE FORM OF STORYTELLING.
FROM THE ULTIMATE STORYTELLER.

ABOUT THE AUTHORS

JAMES PATTERSON is one of the best-known and biggest-selling writers of all time. His books have sold in excess of 325 million copies worldwide. He is the author of some of the most popular series of the past two decades – the Alex Cross, Women's Murder Club, Detective Michael Bennett and Private novels – and he has written many other number one bestsellers including romance novels and stand-alone thrillers.

James is passionate about encouraging children to read. Inspired by his own son who was a reluctant reader, he also writes a range of books for young readers including the Middle School, I Funny, Treasure Hunters, House of Robots, Confessions, and Maximum Ride series. James has donated millions in grants to independent bookshops and has been the most borrowed author in UK libraries for the past ten years in a row. He lives in Florida with his wife and son.

Find out more at www.jamespatterson.co.uk.

Become a fan of James Patterson on Facebook

RICHARD DiLALLO is a former advertising executive. He lives in Manhattan with his wife.

Murder Games

James Patterson
& Howard Roughan

A serial killer is loose on the streets of Manhattan.

His victims appear to be total strangers. The only clue that links the crimes is the playing card left behind at each scene that hints at the next target.

The killer, known in the tabloids as The Dealer, is baiting cops into a deadly guessing game that has the city increasingly on edge. Elizabeth Needham, the tenacious cop in charge of the case, turns to an unlikely ally – Dylan Reinhart, a brilliant professor whose book turned up in connection with the murders.

As the public frenzy over The Dealer reaches a fever pitch, Dylan and Elizabeth must connect the clues to discover what the victims have in common – before The Dealer runs through his entire deck.

CENTURY

AVAILABLE NOW IN HARDBACK

Fifty Fifty

James Patterson
& Candice Fox

**It's not easy being a good detective . . .
when your brother's a serial killer.**

Sam Blue stands accused of the brutal murders of
three young students, their bodies dumped near
the Georges River. Only one person believes he is
innocent: his sister, Detective Harriet Blue. And she's
determined to prove it.

Except she's now been banished to the outback town
of Last Chance Valley (population 75), where a diary
found on the roadside outlines a shocking plan – the
massacre of the entire town. And the first death,
shortly after Harry's arrival, suggests the clock is
already ticking.

Meanwhile, back in Sydney, a young woman holds the
key to crack Sam's case wide open.

**If only she could escape the madman
holding her hostage . . .**

CENTURY

Also by James Patterson

ALEX CROSS NOVELS

Along Came a Spider • Kiss the Girls • Jack and Jill • Cat and Mouse • Pop Goes the Weasel • Roses are Red • Violets are Blue • Four Blind Mice • The Big Bad Wolf • London Bridges • Mary, Mary • Cross • Double Cross • Cross Country • Alex Cross's Trial (*with Richard DiLallo*) • I, Alex Cross • Cross Fire • Kill Alex Cross • Merry Christmas, Alex Cross • Alex Cross, Run • Cross My Heart • Hope to Die • Cross Justice • Cross the Line

THE WOMEN'S MURDER CLUB SERIES

1st to Die • 2nd Chance (*with Andrew Gross*) • 3rd Degree (*with Andrew Gross*) • 4th of July (*with Maxine Paetro*) • The 5th Horseman (*with Maxine Paetro*) • The 6th Target (*with Maxine Paetro*) • 7th Heaven (*with Maxine Paetro*) • 8th Confession (*with Maxine Paetro*) • 9th Judgement (*with Maxine Paetro*) • 10th Anniversary (*with Maxine Paetro*) • 11th Hour (*with Maxine Paetro*) • 12th of Never (*with Maxine Paetro*) • Unlucky 13 (*with Maxine Paetro*) • 14th Deadly Sin (*with Maxine Paetro*) • 15th Affair (*with Maxine Paetro*) • 16th Seduction (*with Maxine Paetro*)

DETECTIVE MICHAEL BENNETT SERIES

Step on a Crack (*with Michael Ledwidge*) • Run for Your Life (*with Michael Ledwidge*) • Worst Case (*with Michael Ledwidge*) • Tick Tock (*with Michael Ledwidge*) • I, Michael Bennett (*with Michael Ledwidge*) • Gone (*with Michael Ledwidge*) • Burn (*with Michael Ledwidge*) • Alert (*with Michael Ledwidge*) • Bullseye (*with Michael Ledwidge*)

PRIVATE NOVELS

Private (*with Maxine Paetro*) • Private London (*with Mark Pearson*) • Private Games (*with Mark Sullivan*) • Private: No. 1 Suspect (*with Maxine Paetro*) • Private Berlin (*with Mark Sullivan*) • Private Down Under (*with Michael White*) • Private L.A. (*with Mark Sullivan*) • Private India (*with Ashwin Sanghi*) • Private Vegas (*with Maxine Paetro*) • Private Sydney (*with Kathryn Fox*) • Private Paris (*with Mark Sullivan*) • The Games (*with Mark Sullivan*) • Private Delhi (*with Ashwin Sanghi*)

NYPD RED SERIES

NYPD Red (*with Marshall Karp*) • NYPD Red 2 (*with Marshall Karp*) • NYPD Red 3 (*with Marshall Karp*) • NYPD Red 4 (*with Marshall Karp*)

DETECTIVE HARRIET BLUE SERIES

Never Never (*with Candice Fox*) • Fifty Fifty (*with Candice Fox*)

NON-FICTION

Torn Apart (*with Hal and Cory Friedman*) • The Murder of King Tut (*with Martin Dugard*)

ROMANCE

Sundays at Tiffany's (*with Gabrielle Charbonnet*) • The Christmas Wedding (*with Richard DiLallo*) • First Love (*with Emily Raymond*) • Two from the Heart (*with Frank Costantini, Emily Raymond and Brian Sitts*)

OTHER TITLES

Miracle at Augusta (*with Peter de Jonge*)

FAMILY OF PAGE-TURNERS

MIDDLE SCHOOL BOOKS

The Worst Years of My Life (*with Chris Tebbetts*) • Get Me Out of Here! (*with Chris Tebbetts*) • My Brother Is a Big, Fat Liar (*with Lisa Papademetriou*) • How I Survived Bullies, Broccoli, and Snake Hill (*with Chris Tebbetts*) • Ultimate Showdown (*with Julia Bergen*) • Save Rafe! (*with Chris Tebbetts*) • Just My Rotten Luck (*with Chris Tebbetts*) • Dog's Best Friend (*with Chris Tebbetts*) • Escape to Australia (*with Martin Chatterton*)

I FUNNY SERIES

I Funny (*with Chris Grabenstein*) • I Even Funnier (*with Chris Grabenstein*) • I Totally Funniest (*with Chris Grabenstein*) • I Funny TV (*with Chris Grabenstein*) • School of Laughs (*with Chris Grabenstein*)

TREASURE HUNTERS SERIES

Treasure Hunters (*with Chris Grabenstein*) • Danger Down the Nile (*with Chris Grabenstein*) • Secret of the Forbidden City (*with Chris Grabenstein*) • Peril at the Top of the World (*with Chris Grabenstein*)

HOUSE OF ROBOTS SERIES

House of Robots (*with Chris Grabenstein*) • Robots Go Wild! (*with Chris Grabenstein*) • Robot Revolution (*with Chris Grabenstein*)

OTHER ILLUSTRATED NOVELS

Kenny Wright: Superhero (*with Chris Tebbetts*) • Homeroom Diaries (*with Lisa Papademetriou*) • Jacky Ha-Ha (*with Chris Grabenstein*) • Word of Mouse (*with Chris Grabenstein*) • Pottymouth and Stoopid (*with Chris Grabenstein*)

MAXIMUM RIDE SERIES

The Angel Experiment • School's Out Forever • Saving the World and Other Extreme Sports • The Final Warning • Max • Fang • Angel • Nevermore • Forever

CONFESSIONS SERIES

Confessions of a Murder Suspect (*with Maxine Paetro*) • The Private School Murders (*with Maxine Paetro*) • The Paris Mysteries (*with Maxine Paetro*) • The Murder of an Angel (*with Maxine Paetro*)

WITCH & WIZARD SERIES

Witch & Wizard (*with Gabrielle Charbonnet*) • The Gift (*with Ned Rust*) • The Fire (*with Jill Dembowski*) • The Kiss (*with Jill Dembowski*) • The Lost (*with Emily Raymond*)

DANIEL X SERIES

The Dangerous Days of Daniel X (*with Michael Ledwidge*) • Watch the Skies (*with Ned Rust*) • Demons and Druids (*with Adam Sadler*) • Game Over (*with Ned Rust*) • Armageddon (*with Chris Grabenstein*) • Lights Out (*with Chris Grabenstein*)

OTHER TITLES

Cradle and All • Crazy House (*with Gabrielle Charbonnet*)

GRAPHIC NOVELS

Daniel X: Alien Hunter (*with Leopoldo Gout*) • Maximum Ride: Manga Vols. 1–9 (*with NaRae Lee*)

For more information about James Patterson's novels, visit www.jamespatterson.co.uk

Or become a fan on Facebook